Marty Dickson was born in a small market village called Sixmilecross, in the county of Tyrone, Northern Ireland, and spent all of his youth living there. He started to write music at the age of fifteen and played his first live gig at the age of seventeen. His love for Rock music and Motorcycles was to become his passion in life. In 1987, he moved to Cambridge with his then-girlfriend, Elaine, who he married ten years after the day they met. He played Bass guitar in numerous bands over the years, spending most of his time on the road touring or in his studio, writing and recording music. He had some success with one of his songs entering the Top 100 singles charts. He also became a keen restorer of old motorcycles, which he owes to his father, Cecil Dickson, who was an ex Road Racer and restorer himself. In 2015, he decided to give up on the constant touring and recording, and turn to writing books. This is his first book to be released. He has never forgotten his hometown and writes passionately about his love for it. With his second novel underway, Sixmilecross will yet again play a role in it. He still lives with his wife and children in Cambridge, England.

Dedicated to all the forgotten, innocent victims of the troubles in Ulster, who seem to be the only ones who have paid the price for peace.
And still are.

Marty Dickson

ALL FOR THE LOVE OF A FATHER

AUSTIN MACAULEY PUBLISHERS™

LONDON • CAMBRIDGE • NEW YORK • SHARJAH

A CIP catalogue record for this title is available from the British Library.

ISBN 9781528911672 (Paperback)
ISBN 9781528911689 (Kindle e-book)
ISBN 9781528959865 (ePub e-book)

From this point onward this book is a work of fiction. Any names or characters, businesses or places, events or incidents, are fictitious. Any resemblance to actual persons, living or dead, or actual events is purely coincidental.

www.austinmacauley.com

First Published (2019)
Austin Macauley Publishers Ltd
25 Canada Square
Canary Wharf
London
E14 5LQ

My thanks goes to the W. F. Marshall family for letting me use a verse from *Tullyneil* in my first book. My father was a great lover of his work and grew up in Drumlister, which was the influence to another one of his poems, *Me an'me Da*, which is all about living in Drumlister. That is the link my father's family has with Sixmilecross and W. F. Marshall. If you ever get the chance to visit Tyrone, find your way to Sixmilecross. The history of W. F. Marshall is everywhere to see.

I have to thank my three girls, who encouraged me through the writing of this book. My wonderful wife, Elaine; and our beautiful daughters, Lisa-Ann and Kerrie-Louise, I owe you and love you so much.

Finally, to the families of all the innocent victims. Never let your voices be silenced, because your voices are the voices of the innocent victims of terrorism in Ulster.

Contents

Prologue

To a lot of people in Ulster, the peace was welcome, but some people openly accuse both the British and Irish governments of trying to 'airbrush history' to cover up deaths to appease the victim makers. Those people are the victims who have and always will be the only ones to pay the price for peace in Ulster. Every family and every person in the north of Ireland has been affected by the troubles in some way. Through the generations of the last century, Catholics and Protestants have been at war with each other, with the British government in the middle. Some hoped that this would all change when peace was agreed in 1921. Nearly all the sides agreed on a ceasefire and a way forward. Some didn't and vowed to carry on fighting to get the brits out of Ireland no matter how long it took. The six counties of Ulster stayed within the British Empire and the remaining twenty-six counties stayed part of the Republic of Ireland. From this time forward, Catholics and Protestants began to live side by side in peace and in some cases Protestants and Catholics married. Strong family ties between the two religions meant that the old divisions became more and more distant. My mother's parents were from that time. My grandfather, a Protestant man, and my grandmother, a Catholic woman, started a family hoping that the peace would hold and their different religions would never again divide people. Forward fifty years, this was still the case, but the peace was broken.

Now, Catholics and Protestants were being harassed for, as it was called, shagging the other side. If you did, you were a Taig-lover or a proddy-lover, and in some cases, people were badly beaten and even murdered for doing so. My grandparents stuck together through thick and thin but they and their children, because of pressure from the troubles began to take different sides in the conflict. My parents followed in my grandparents' footsteps and married the other side. Daddy was a Protestant and Mummy a Catholic. It became very hard for them, day to day, with the instigators of the troubles on both sides of the divide trying to make their ideals the local law. Thankfully, my parents didn't listen to anything but their hearts. With the troubles in full force again, more and more innocent people from both sides got caught up in it and were made to take sides. Some did and were happy to. Some had no choice but to do what they were told and those who were left did what was right and stood up to the gangs of murders. For that, they became some of the innocent victims. Both sides murdered anyone who went against their beliefs and both sides killed at will. As a family, we were one of those innocent families who become victims of the troubles. A mixed family, with both Protestant and Catholic relations, we inadvertently become a target. We lost so much in the blink of an eye and none of this was our own doing. The terrorists become more and more vicious without a care to the one's whose lives would be destroyed for ever. The shootings become endless and without a second thought and the bombings become relentless and indiscriminate. Thousands died and tens of thousands were affected beyond belief. To us, it was like the end of the world and to them, it was just another job well done.

Former US senator George Mitchell:

"Nobody can expect those who lost a loved one to let go of their grief. That's human, natural and understandable, but in the end, Northern Ireland has made a decision to move forward and it was a right decision, whatever the consequences of the past."

Chapter 1
Mummy's Goodbye

Standing in a churchyard in the far corner of a small County Tyrone market village, commonly called the Cross, is where our life's journey, that started some 25 years ago, ended. It's not a journey we took willingly; it's a journey forced upon us because of someone else's ideology. This churchyard at the edge of the village is a place that is so quiet and peaceful. A place you would think would be free from the disease and hatred that is destroying the land we love, yet it's full of the results of that disease and hatred that has destroyed every stretch, every corner and every piece of this land that you step on and every single person you see or speak to carried the burden of grief forced upon them.

Wherever I look in this beautiful graveyard, there are the reminders of that disease and hatred buried below in the ground that I tread.

The wind blows through the trees making a sound that, in my mind, could be heard nowhere else. The old oak trees move side to side in the swift breeze and you can imagine what has passed them by in the old, gone and forgotten days and if they could speak what tales and woes they would tell.

The birds are singing and seem to be flying above us in sync, flying in tandem to the sound of the wind on the branches and leaves and swooping down towards us as if they were about to attack us before flying upwards again. In the distance you can see the Sperrin Mountains and the green grass on the hills and fields. And all the different colours of the trees blowing in the breeze are like a painter's dream scene. I can imagine a painter like James Humbert Craig, originally from Belfast, spend his life time looking for such natural beauty and also where a local poet called W.F Marshall got his inspiration from to write some of his best-known poems. Reverend William Forbes Marshall was an Ulster poet and Presbyterian Minister in the Cross. He was Daddy's favourite poet and he would often recite his poems to us. As I make my way round the church, I stop at the large stained-glass window commemorating Jesus Christ. It was done by the Dunlap family, one of whom, John Dunlap, printed the United States Declaration of Independence. It's amazing to think that such a small village in Tyrone has a link to such a moment in time. I keep walking on round, stopping at the graves of people I once knew to pay my respects. It seems to take me longer each time. As the years pass by and people get older, they soon take their place here. A place I will take when my time comes. At the back of the church, way down below in the valley, there's a river that snakes its way through the fields.

Usually in the evenings you would see a man out fly fishing after a day's work. Daddy spent many an evening on that river, trying to catch enough to feed eight mouths. No doubt he needed the time alone to relax. I can see the remanence of the old unused railway line that use to run through the village. It opened in 1863 and closed in 1965, but I can still imagine the steam trains tearing across the valley, steam pumping through the spout as it makes its way through the countryside. Dad told us the joy he had taking the train when he was a young boy. His dad used to take them all on the train just to get to the next village. It was the highlight of their summer. I remember playing on the rails as a child with my brothers and Daddy, chasing the rabbits up and down the lines but never being able to catch them.

On one occasion, we were trying to find a good railway sleeper so that Dad could finish off the old fireplace in the house. It was so much fun running along trying to find the best sleeper so that you could be the one to say I found the sleeper. When we did find the one, the fun was trying to carry it back the whole way to the house. We laughed and laughed at each other when we tripped over or just couldn't do it. It made me smile thinking back and imagining us enjoying our childhood as all children should. As the clouds move in the breeze, you can see the darkness fall in the valley but only for a moment before the sun breaks through again and the green of the land takes your breath away again and again.

I can see the cars and tractors in the distance moving along the small country roads between the hedges and cows slowly move around the fields eating away at grass without a care. Then, all of a sudden, you'd get the smell of the countryside as the local farmers start working their lands and spreading manure on the fields. Some people hate that smell and I'm sure I did when I was a child, but now when I do smell the farmers working away, I love it. It kind of brings me back to happier days. Then, before you know it, the stench of the muck spreading has passed and it all changes again.

That's how quick the landscape changes and the pace of life moves around the small Tyrone village.

Now there's a smell of freshly-cut grass in the graveyard as the caretaker starts his weekly chores which brings out the bees looking for flowers to have a feast. All around are white butterflies which always remind me of a loved one who passed. The deafening silence at times always bring a sense of relaxation and makes me think again of happier times and happier days. But those happier days have been few and far between.

This churchyard is a place that, as a young boy, I loved to go to and just think of things. Things that have passed us by and us not being able to do anything about it, things that would drive us down a road, a road that no one in their right mind would ever want to go down and also thinking of what the future holds for us all. I would always call this place my place of peace. If I ever needed to get away from life in general, I would visit this place in my mind, in my dreams or in person, if at all possible. I would always feel a sense of peace and freedom that no one could take from me. It was my own corner of the world that I could rely on.

I would lie on the grass, when it was dry, that is, and look up at the clouds moving across a beautiful blue sky. It was not often blue but when it was, it took your breath away.

The odd time, a pheasant or maybe a duck would fly past in between the endless crows and rooks and that would excite the hell out of me; as a young boy, things like that would excite you. All around me the world keeps moving, but for me, it's like time's standing still. Other kids would be playing together in parks and laughing without a care in the world. For my brothers and me, that was not the case. We were in a world of sorrow and loneliness, where the only ones we could rely on was ourselves. It was something that never really left us. We just found a dark corner to put all that sorrow and loneliness in when we needed to.

We have always had a big black hole in our world, and no matter what, we just could not seem to get out of it. It feels like we have always been on the outside looking in. Not that as kids we didn't try. It just seemed that we were different, different in many ways; there were other families in our position but that was them. We still felt different than everyone else.

Where to begin?

I think in this case maybe where it ended, for the ending was the beginning of the rest of our lives. On a cold winter's morning, we finally got the chance to bury the past, only it was filled with real sadness and not relief.

Carrying Mum to her resting place is something we always knew would come, but as children, we never thought of it. As we carry her through the gates of our home for the last time, I get a feeling of emptiness and déjà vu.

We walked arm in arm carrying Mum's coffin the whole way to the church, not giving way to other family members who were willing to take a lift. None of us boys wanted to let her go, and we wanted to stay with her until she was finally back with Daddy; only then would we let go. That's just how we felt. As we got closer to the church, we could feel that what went before was coming back to us. It never seemed to leave.

It was like we were constantly being dragged back to the same spot in time.

We carried Mummy through parts of the graveyard and past the same faces we did before on a few occasions. We stopped at the doors before taking a deep breath. Then we walked into a full church of friends and family and people who just wanted to say goodbye to a one-of-a-kind woman. The choice of music we picked seemed to be the only one that was fitting enough for Mum. There's a New Star in Heaven Tonight by Chris de Burgh. Why, because that's what she was to us, a bright star that would do anything for us.

As we got to the altar, the reverend was there, ready to receive Mum into this house of God. We lowered her down, then stood and waited until the end of the song and only then did we make our way to our families in the front rows. It all fell quiet for what felt like an eternity but was only minutes. The reason, Reverend Brown was saying a prayer privately to Mum. It was like he was talking to her, letting her know how much she was loved in his own way. As I sat in our church, I looked around as I did so many times before at the plaques on the walls of the local victims of the troubles in my beloved home of Ulster. I saw the faces of people I knew growing up, all my dad's brothers and sisters. I saw some of Mum's brothers and sisters as well, all feeling the pain as we did and so many of our cousins sitting with their parents and of course Mummy's friends, all with sadness in their hearts.

But most of all, I saw the pain and sadness etched on the faces of friends and family. I also saw the never-ending pain on the faces of people that have been victims of the troubles, and no doubt they will look and feel the same way for the rest of their God-given lives. On my left was a plaque of the father of one of my friends growing up. He was shot to death by cowards hiding in a ditch outside his house. Cyril was a quiet man who joined the UDR part-time to, "as he saw it", protect his family. He was leaving home to do his day job when two gunmen jumped out of the ditch and shot him in the back and head from behind. They couldn't face him and look him in the eyes, just like the cowards that they were. They did the same thing to his brother-in-law.

They walked up behind him and took his life without a care for the man or his family.

On my right was the plaque of a local milkman and part-time UDR man who was murdered on his way home from his work when yet again the cowards jumped out of the ditch and shot him dead. But the way they killed him was so, so shocking.

On his way home, he approached a series of bends on the road. As he come up to the first turn, a gunman hiding behind the hedge opened automatic gunfire on the car. He was hit but made it round that first corner only to be hit with another burst from a second gunman. He was hit numerous times but made it to the third turn where the third gunman finished him off. To finish him off, they set light to his milk van. This would not be the last time they carried out such an evil plan. He was known as a strong man who was well known as a gentle giant of a man with not one enemy. He always had a smile on his face and spent his whole adult life as our local milkman.

The plaque that never leaves our thoughts when we go to Church is the plaque in front of us; it is our daddy's. He was a man that Boyd and John never really got to know. They can only just remember little things, very little of what he was like as a dad. Boyd was 3 years old and John 5 years old when his life was taken. Mum and Dad had seven children, all boys. Mum always wanted a girl but it was not to be. One boy was stillborn at birth, which left the six of us. We will never get over that day back in 1979. It never leaves us, and I'm sure it's the same for every family who have gone through the same as us.

He was taken from us by men who thought the only way to get what they wanted was to kill as many Protestants as possible and then make the rest leave. They called themselves freedom fighters of the IRA, but all they were terrorists and murderers of men, women and children.

Me, I remember Dad as a big, strong, fit man who never took a step back, who always spoke his mind and would take the belt to us if we ever stepped out of line, and in a family of six boys, that happened quite frequently.

As we listen to the service for Mum, we are all thinking of her, knowing that she is now back in the arms of the only man she ever loved. She never met another man after Dad was taken from us and she spent the rest of her life devoted to her boys. She was a one-of-a-kind lady who lived her life in lonely sadness. She tried to hide it for the sake of her boys, but now and then she had no choice but to let go of her emotions. That is something we never got over.

To see the pain on her face and hear the pain in her cries was an awful thing—something we would see and hear every night before we would go to sleep. In the morning, she would be ready to do her job as a mother and tried to show us happiness to start the day. We can't and never will get over the lonely nights lying in bed listening to Mummy cry herself to sleep. We all cried with her in our own beds, and on many occasions, I would get up to be with Mummy only to find one or two of us sitting outside her door, crying but not going in. Only difference for us was, we had a brother to turn to. Not one of us could hold it in.

As the service ended, we all got up and made our way to the altar. We stood around her with Reverend Brown. His back was to the people when he spoke to us quietly.

"For the sacrifices you all made for the love of your parents, I commend you. I pray that now you can go forward in life with God in your hearts, knowing that you did what you had to do out of pure and unbroken love. May God bless you all and may God receive your mother into heaven to be with your father once again. I say this in the name of Jesus Christ our Lord. Amen."

We picked up Mum and began the last walk to her resting place. The tears started to blind us but there was no way we were going to let that stop us. We carried her out, standing tall into the sunshine, knowing that Daddy was waiting for her on the other side. Mum's favourite song "Stand by Your Man" accompanied her home, and as we left the church, we as one knew she was going to a happier place, to be with our daddy.

Standing at what felt like the edge of the earth again was in fact a dark hole in a graveyard. We were about to say our final goodbye to the only person we looked up to and would do anything to help and protect. Mum was the backbone of our family. She had a hard start in life and it never seemed to get any better. She never complained or never showed us any of the pain she endured.

Our mum was so special, the most special, kind, loving woman that anyone could ever meet or know. She passed away of a broken heart nearly 25 years after it had been broken, but we have no doubt she was looking forward to meeting her only love in the afterlife. That was her only blessing in her last days. She said to us in her last days that it felt like Daddy was calling her home.

Standing at the graveside, I found myself mentally go into a world that I began to rely on again and again and not for the first time it helped me through. While in my place of peace, I started to ask myself: "How did we get here?"

It's been a journey that destroyed our family like so many others on this island of Ulster. It has left a void that could never be filled. No matter what we did or what we tried to fill that void with, it always seemed to be empty the next day.

The thing is, it was not of our making; it's just something we had to deal with and try to carry on the best we could. No matter what though, it always came back to haunt us, and it just would not go away. When we tried to turn the corner, we always seemed to hit a brick wall and the only thing to do was to get up and bounce back, but with six boys, there is no doubt we were all going to be different, and we were in many, many ways. It was just a matter of try and try again to get over whatever wall we confronted. Christmas was never the same after Dad died. He was taken on the 10th of December 1979. We got to learn very quickly that Santa Claus was only a story that was passed down from parents to their children at Christmas time. I do remember the joys of Christmas morning, waking up to find that Santa had left us presents, though John and Boyd don't have such memories. It was never the same, even though the presents still appeared under the Christmas tree on Christmas morning.

The smiles on everyone's faces were gone. Even the younger of us knew the pain of not having Dad with us. Mummy did her best to make it as special as possible but we could never remove the memory of what happened two weeks before Christmas day in 1979.

Chapter 2
Family Life

Like nearly every family in Ulster, life has been interrupted by troubles in some way. Catholics and Protestants alike suffered at the hands of terrorists from both sides. Some families suffered worse than others, but the pain was always the same to us all. There were no winners, only losers at the end of every day and usually there was some sort of terrorist attack on a daily basis; some family somewhere would have their worlds turned upside down in a moment. It could be in the north, the south or the mainland. It could happen to anyone, anywhere.

We grew up in a unique, small farming village called The Cross. It had one main street, one post office, one butcher, two shops and three pubs. We had two churches and one primary school. I would say that it was a 50/50 split on religion and we seemed to get along at the best of times, but when times got bad and things happened, people seem to take sides. This was usually Catholic or Protestant. Mummy lived in the next village and was one of 10 siblings. Six girls and four boys. They were brought up Catholics. Her dad, Grandad D, was a Protestant man and my Granny D was a Catholic woman. When they met, religion was still as big an issue as it is today, but they seemed to overcome that. Mind you, you wouldn't think that with some of the things that went on in later years. Back in those days, as it still is today, it was a sin to marry the other side. Some did and some never forgave those who did.

Dad, on the other hand, grew up in a Protestant family outside the Cross on a small farm. He was one of eight siblings, six boys and two girls. I guess you could say they never had TVs to occupy themselves in the late nights back in those days. Mum and Dad met through our grandad. He knew Dad way before Dad met Mum. Their love of old farm tractors was how they met.

Daddy would take grandad's tractors to meetings and shows. He ended up helping Grandad repair and restore his old tractor. Grandad was a farmer as well. Mummy would sometimes go with grandad to the meetings and, of course, Daddy would be always there. When Daddy would call at Grandad's house to work on the tractors, Mummy would always make up an excuse to get out to the big shed to see Daddy. It was usually making tea that would do the job. At one meeting, Daddy asked Grandad if he could court mummy; he said yes. That was the beginning of our family and the rest was history.

Mum's mum, Granny D, on the other hand, didn't like it at all. She became a strong, deep, religious woman who never made a secret of her thoughts and beliefs. She would force all her children down the road of being reared in the Roman Catholic religion. She would do anything to make sure Mummy and Daddy would not be able to meet up or see each other. Daddy was not welcome around Grandad's home anymore because of the relationship. Anytime they did meet up, it was always in secret. It was most definitely forbidden love. I think they courted for six months before they were found out, and when Granny D did find out, she was none too pleased. Mummy said they had a massive row one night, and at the end, Mummy walked out of the house and never looked back. She made her way to Daddy's house and the whole family welcomed her with open arms. They were not allowed to sleep together. That's one thing Granny R would not accept under her roof. Mummy slept in the same room as the girls in the house but I'm sure they sneaked a bit of time together. Not long into their courtship, and when it was now in the open, Granny D sent two local IRA men out to Daddy's home to take Mummy home and warn Daddy off. Uncle Jimmy was the one to answer the door, and when he did, he didn't know what to think. Two hooded men at his door ordering him around. That soon went very wrong indeed. Dad was one of six boys who all had a bit of a reputation with their fists and were not found wanting when trouble came at them. Now in those days, it was different than today. Today, people never use their fists. They use some sort of tool. In Daddy's day, their fists did the talking and by all accounts, he could talk.

"We have come here for Rose Darcy so get her out here now or we come in and get her."

Uncle Jimmy just stood there in disbelief for a moment before looking at them and saying, "What do you want with her?"

They stepped forward in an aggressive manor and replied, "We have come to take her home where she belongs and tell your brother to stay clear of her. We will only warn him once."

At that point, Uncle Jimmy said, "Wait a minute," and closed the door. He stood there in complete shock for a moment only to reappear soon after with a shotgun. At this point, they were the ones in complete shock. "You have ten seconds to get the fuck off our land, and if you don't, you're both going to get a barrel in the face or back if you want. You're used to that, aren't you?" As he raised the gun, the two men ran like hell down the lane and into their car. People like that are cowards when faced with the same fate they try to force on others. They are usually the ones to shoot people in the back and never face on. Seconds later, when Dad appeared to see what all the noise was about, Uncle Jimmy informed him what just occurred. He was livid at the idea of two IRA men thinking they could get away with such a thing. He jumped on his motorcycle and chased after them. It was late at night so Dad followed with his lights off so he could find out who they were.

He followed them for about 10 minutes to a house he knew quite well, only to find that they were talking to Granny D outside her house. He then followed them to find out who they were and where they lived. That didn't take long. He knew of them through being with grandad at the tractor meetings. He made his way back home and just bided his time to get his revenge. He said nothing at the time to Mum, not wanting to upset her. It would be quite difficult explaining to a girl what her mother just did. To make her believe it would be another issue. In the following months, Daddy caught up with the two known IRA men one at a time. Needless to say, they got just rewards with a good thumping. One of them turned out to be one of Mummy's uncles. Daddy was too smart to take on the IRA men when they wore the mask of a terrorist.

He waited until an opportunity arose, and when it did, he went at it. He had backup just in case though, in the shape of five brothers. He made it look like a normal bar fight so as not to have the IRA try to get revenge and kill him or his family. The brothers were not needed, though, as Daddy was one hell of a scrapper. He had fast and heavy fists and knew how to use them. In later years, when I met my first and serious girlfriend, Maggie the first thing her mum said to me when we first met was, "Are you anything to the fighting Richards from the Cross?" Knowing of the stories from Daddy's past and the reputation he and his brothers had, I had to say yes. Even going back to my Grandad R's time and his family, they also had a hard men reputation, so it runs in the family.

Although times were hard for families back then, it didn't stop them having large families. Some say they tried to outbreed each other so that when the war came they would have the largest army of voices behind them. It's the same story today, only its more votes as well as they try and outdo each other.

When Mummy and Daddy decided to get married, they had no help from anyone, so he had to sell his tractor to help pay for it. Those days most couples eloped to Scotland to get married. Mummy and Daddy did just that. They sold everything they could to get the money to elope to Gretna Green and get married. I don't know how long they spent in Scotland but I'm sure they knew that when they returned they would damn sure not be welcomed back into their family circle. We know that was not the case with Daddy's family. They accepted Mummy with open arms, although I'm sure there was some hesitance at first. When they returned, they were immediately and completely out-casted by all of Mummy's family.

I remember, as a young boy, while in the next village to the Cross, meeting Granny D in the village. She crossed the road just so she wouldn't have to speak to me. I also remember meeting one of my aunts on the bus. I was walking past the bus she was on and what she did to me is something I will always remember. It was a simple 'fuck you' gesture. Saying that, we would most likely do the same back if need be but not to Mummy's sister.

Dad got the chance to rent a house outside the Cross to begin their life together and to raise a family. It was simple: two bedrooms, kitchen and an outside toilet. Heating was an open fire. At first, they had no electric and had to use Tilley lamps. It wasn't a big deal as they had to use them when growing up in their family homes. They had an old Aga stove to cook their food which again they were used to growing up. They had no car at first but Daddy did get himself a little Royal Enfield to get to work. He worked in a local tractor garage part time as well as on his dad's farm, earning enough to look after them both, but it wasn't long before mummy got pregnant with their first child. Within a year of getting married, they had their first child. In 1966, their first boy was born. They named him James. He was the first-born male into the Richards family. Granny and Grandad R were over the moon, but nothing come from Granny D. Some of Mummy's brothers and sisters did, however, congratulate them. They did it in secret though because Granny D would not take kindly to them saying anything to them or even acknowledge that they had a nephew. Things got a bit harder for them, and the troubles in Ulster started to gather pace. Mummy could not rely on much help from her family even though some of them did try. Some of her sisters did stay in touch but Granny D would never do so. Grandad D seemed to show some interest in us boys, but he only ever showed it in private. One of Mummy's sisters, Aunty Mary, did, however, get caught by Granny D having contact with Mummy. She found some baby clothes in her room at their home, and when she was asked about them, she told Granny D that they were for Mummy. They had a massive row and Aunty Mary left home. She was now in the same boat as Mummy. Dad's family were their only reliable help but only because of the first grandson born in the family. Most of the time, they were on their own. It wasn't long before they had another child on the way, and late in 1967, they had another son. They named him Sammy. Sammy had to stay in hospital for a short while because of complications, but after a few months, he was fine and was very healthy. Again, Granny D did not want to know anything about them. On one occasion, they met in the Cross by chance, and Granny D decided to give Mummy a piece of her mind. Mummy was so upset, she cried on the street in front of the whole village.

"Who the hell do you think you are, swanning around with those proddy bastards' children? You should be ashamed of yourself, you wee bitch. Look at the cut of you. You're nothing but a bloody slapper, and you're no daughter of mine anymore." As she walked away she shouted back, "And stay away from your brothers and sisters. If I ever see you anywhere near any of them, I'll batter you stupid."

She walked away, leaving Mummy in tears in the middle of the Cross with two young babies. She felt ashamed with all the people looking at them. Some people, who had seen what happened, came to Mummy's aid and helped her calm down. Word soon spread about the Cross on what happened and Granny D got a swift, sharp response from the local community. Everywhere she went, people would point at her and whisper about her behind her back. Some people talked about the local priest visiting her to convey his displeasure. For Granny D, this—if true—would worry her as she was a devout Roman Catholic, but she never changed her ways. The other times that it happened, Granny D made sure that it was done where no one would hear or see it happen. When Daddy found out, Mummy begged him not to do anything that would make things worse than they already were. Daddy was livid, though, and decided to find Grandad D to find out what the hell is going on. When he eventually did meet up with Grandad D, it turned out that he was unaware of how bad it was. He did hear about the confrontation on the Cross street through some people at his work and he was none too pleased to say the least. He did tell Daddy that he would deal with it and that such a thing would never happen again. Daddy made him promise not to let Mummy know about the meeting. We don't know what was said to Granny D, but things settled down between the families.

The year was now 1969 and Mummy was about to have another new born and had just moved into a house in the Cross. It had electric, an indoor bathroom, proper heating and, most importantly for Mummy, neighbours. Things had settled down and seemed to be in the past. Some of Mummy's brothers and sisters were now on speaking terms with them, despite what Granny D said in 1967. Daddy was back to helping Grandad D with his tractors but not at Granny D's house. This is the year I was brought into the world and a year that saw the start of the troubles in the North of Ireland. Rioting become commonplace in Londonderry and Belfast through the summer of 1969, which also saw the first deaths of the troubles conflict. An Apprentice Boys' march in Londonderry on 12 August sparked rioting in the Catholic 'Bogside' area, which led to two days of serious violence. Violence then broke out across Northern Ireland. The North's government at Stormont requested that the British Army be sent in to help restore order but only as a brief intervention. At first, the British Army was welcomed but that soon changed. The British Army soon become the target and the enemy of every Catholic in Northern Ireland. The British Army would not leave the North and its troubles until 2007. Operation Banner was the operational name for the British Armed Forces' operation in Northern Ireland. Not a perfect world to be born into, but I wasn't the only one. I was named Stephen and I was the 3rd born boy. Mummy was wanting a baby girl at this stage, but she didn't care as long as the baby was healthy. I had the blessing of being born into a nice home with all the mod cons. James and Sammy never had that luxury when they were born. Mummy always said, despite the break out of rioting and the troubles in the north of Ireland, that Christmas was one of the best the family had. A new start in a new house with a new born baby. Christmas felt like Christmas. I can only imagine what Christmas was like in an old house in the country with no electric and no one close by, but knowing Mummy and Daddy, they would not let it get to them and always make the most of what they had.

In 1970, with the troubles gaining momentum, the Ulster Defence Regiment (UDR), an infantry regiment of the British Army, was established. Their official role was the defence of life and property in Northern Ireland against armed attack or sabotage. That role soon changed when the troubles become widespread through the North of Ireland.

At the end of 1970, Daddy was doing so well at his work the elderly owner of the tractor business asked him to become a co-owner and to run the place in his absence. He was getting on in age and didn't want the business to fold. He had no sons or daughters to pass it on to. Daddy seemed to be the perfect man for the job. Our lives got better from that point as Daddy got more pay for the job he was doing. Before long, Mummy and Daddy could afford to buy a house. They did so outside the Cross. They bought a nice house with a bit of land and a farm barn on the edge. That was something Daddy always wanted—somewhere to put his old tractors so that he could work on them in his spare time. That also meant that Grandad D would visit us which meant a lot to Mummy. He did get into a lot of arguments with Granny D over his visits to the new house though. In 1970, with the troubles in full force, Mummy had another child and yet again it was another baby boy. They named him Billy after Grandad R. Thankfully the house was big enough for a family of six. We had plenty of land to play around in and some farm yard animals to keep us company. In 1971, Daddy took a decision to join the newly formed British Army, the Ulster Defence Regiment (UDR). He felt that it was time to step up and protect firstly the Protestant community and also to defend the citizens of Northern Ireland. He wasn't the only one in the Cross area to do so. Nearly every Protestant family had a son or daughter join up. Daddy had two other bothers join up as well. Back in the early seventies, it was so bad in Ulster every family was in some way affected—Catholic and Protestant. In the year of 1972, Mummy got pregnant again. She had another baby boy but this time the same complications Mummy had with Sammy happened again. This time it took the life of Mummy's 5th born. Richie died on the 12th of November 1972. Mummy took it bad and took a long time to get over the death of baby Richie, and just when things were settled on the family front with Granny D, she started again. When she heard of the death of Mummy's 5th child, she couldn't wait to have her say. This time it wasn't directly to Mummy but to Aunty Mary. Aunty Mary was not one to take that sort of crap from anyone, even if it was her mother. She said that Mummy and Daddy deserved all they got. From what we are told, Aunty Mary give her quite a touch back. It took a couple of years for Mummy and Daddy to get over their loss of baby Richie and while they tried to come to terms with it all around them death and destruction raged on the streets of Ulster.

Although things were good for us, things in 1973 were about to take an awful turn. Daddy had been in the UDR now for 2 years. Even though he was only part time, if you put the part time UDR and working in the tractor garage together, it makes for a long day. Daddy's manner changed a bit. At the start of 1973, we found out why he was changing. One of his friends and colleagues in the UDR was killed in an attack at his home by the IRA. They rushed his house on three sides when he walked out his front door to drive to work. He didn't have a chance. He never even had a chance to get his personal weapon out to shoot back. Daddy took it bad. It was the first of many of UDR men to be assassinated off duty. They never attacked them the same way when they were on duty. Things changed about the house after that. First thing he did was to get a dog. He called the dog Root. He was also more security conscious. He put guns at nearly every exit point at the house. The UDR in our area changed their ways as well. Every one of them got more security conscious. That would not be enough to protect everyone in the coming years. More and more people were losing their lives for no goddamn reason. Day after day, week after week, month after month, good people on both sides died for, and all in the name of, religion. That drove more and more Protestants to join the UDR and in some cases the UVF and more and more Catholics to join the IRA. In 1974, another baby was born into the ever-growing family. Mummy had yet another boy. Still not a baby girl, and that's what she craved. Baby John was the 6th child to be born into the family. With the death of Richie, it meant only five though. Daddy always had a saying when talking about having children. People always said to him that if he keeps going he would have his own football team, but he would always say when he had enough to carry his coffin he would stop. It was only a joke and said in jest, but it turned out to be the case. In 1975, there were some signs of peace when the IRA agreed a ceasefire with the British government. It was during that ceasefire that the terrorist groups started to turn on each other. A feud began between the Official IRA (OIRA) and the Irish National Liberation Army (INLA) and also a feud began between the Ulster Volunteer Force (UVF) and Ulster Defence Association (UDA). Terrorists were killed on both sides. I don't think much sleep was lost over this situation. In 1976, Mummy had her final baby. Was it a boy? Yes, it was. Seven boys in ten years. What were the odds of that? The last baby boy was called Boyd. So the family was set, six boys. James, Sammy, Stephen, Billy, John and Boyd. I was nearly seven when Boyd was born and I remember his first day at home. I remember Daddy carrying him into the house with a big smile on his face and Mummy coming behind with her bags. The first thing she said when she got her shoes off and a cup of tea was: "Right, William you're for the snip now. No more children."

Dad, being old school, said, "Not a hope of that, Rose. That will be your job, love."

Aunty Mary was there and fell in love with Boyd. She had no children of her own but was pregnant with her first child. She was so good to us, and no matter what Granny D thought or said, she did her own thing. The first Christmas we had as a full family was so much fun—there were lots of presents under the Christmas tree and lots of laughter. Mummy and Daddy seemed to be very happy with life and our little family bubble was perfect. Daddy was now the half owner of a good business with good money and Mummy had what she always wanted: a big family around her. The next few years were awful outside of the family life. The terrorists were taking over and running some parts of the country. It was becoming all about money and power and not the percussion of different sides of the community. The terrorist groups were in charge of a lot of areas and you did what they said and gave them what they wanted. If you didn't, you paid the price and usually with your life. We never had much trouble in the Cross but when it did come to the Cross it was big news. Two more of Daddy's friends in the UDR were killed, one on active duty as they were on patrol near the border of the Irish republic and the other as he worked his day job. Daddy took the second murder very badly as it was one of his close friends. I remember the man coming around the house many times whether it was working in the large shed or meeting Daddy for an evening out fishing on the local rivers.

The next four years saw Daddy doing so well at his work that the elderly owner offered Daddy a chance of taking over the business completely. It was such a great offer that Daddy decided to take the chance and take over the business. He made an agreement with the owner to pay off the purchase price in instalments which give him the chance to grow the business. Daddy spread out to farmyard machinery which worked as he also added some new and used machinery for sale. In the past, it was only a repair garage, but it was a very good repair garage. Now Daddy was in charge, he could do what he wanted. First thing he did was to make his brother manager of sales. Uncle Sam was the perfect man for the job. It was around this time that Daddy started taking some of us boys to work with him on a Saturday morning. Although I was too young, I wanted to go but I would have needed fulltime care so Daddy always said no. James and Sammy, on the other hand, went most weekends. James took to it like a duck to water and began to learn a lot about the job. Uncle Sam took him under his wing and began to teach him the ins and outs to do with selling. Sammy seemed to want to spend time on the garage floor with Daddy working on tractors and the farmyard machinery. He always loved to get his hands dirty and often came home covered in grease from head to toe. Mummy was so angry about the build-up of greasy clothes that she got James and Sammy boiler suits. She also got the name of the business on the back of the boiler suits and they loved it. It meant that they would always look after them. She got The Cross Tractors Enterprise Company in big red letters done for them. It was now 1977 and it was a year of more deaths from the troubles. It was getting to a point now that more and more civilians were being killed, a lot more than terrorists. The RUC and UDR were still being targeted and killed as well as the British Army. The IRA started to attack the mainland of England by bombing London and other cities. They didn't care who they killed as long as they left destruction in their wake. In some cases, they let other innocent Irish men take the blame for their actions. Some men spent years in jail for something they didn't do and the IRA never stepped up to help them. Something upset Mummy even more than the troubles. Elvis had just died. Mummy was a big Elvis fan and cried for so long after she heard the news. She always played Elvis records day in and day out singing along the whole time, as did we. You couldn't help but sing along with that voice. I started to spend some of my summer time holidays at Aunty Sally's family home in Enniskillen. I loved spending my time there as it was just like home, only with a lot more farm animals to look after. I looked forward to it all year long. Aunty Sally had a brother the same age as me so we jelled right away. Eddie was a great lad and he became a lifelong friend. Coming to the end of 1977 and everything was great, well only if you ignored the troubles which was quite hard to do with every new day bringing yet more and more deaths. Daddy was now a sergeant in the UDR and had a lot of responsibility both at work and in the UDR. To date, he had lost four members of his unit in terrorist attacks, but I had to say he was getting hardened to losing his friends, but it was still hard to take. The year of 1977 ended with sad news for Mummy. One of her sisters passed away through cancer. It was expected but never easy when it did happen. Aunty Georgina was the eldest of Mummy's family and had a difficult life with leukaemia. It eventually caught up with her in her forties. The other difficult part was Granny D. How would she take meeting Mummy again after years of no contact? We all went to the funeral as a family and not at one time did Granny D say hello to any of us. As far as she was concerned, we didn't exist. We were told not to go into the living room because Granny D would be in there. She had given Grandad D instructions not to let us in sight of her. I remember Aunty Joyce coming up to Mummy and saying, "Don't let her get to you Rose, you know what she's like, you're here for Georgina and to say good bye to her."

That kind of helped Mummy and she felt more at ease. I could see that Daddy was standing in the background waiting just in case something happened. He would have loved to give Granny D a piece of his mind after what had happened when Richie died. All Mummy's brothers and sisters spoke to us without any issues. Uncle Paddy was his usual funny self with us making us laugh and as usual giving us sweets. We stayed for a few hours as Mummy spoke to visitors coming to pay their respects. On the way home, Mummy started to cry saying that it was a hard thing to say goodbye to a sister in that environment. The next day at the funeral, it was the same atmosphere. This time Granny D was at loggerheads with two of her daughters—Mummy and Aunty Mary. We stayed at home with Aunty June who looked after us all day. After the funeral, Mummy and Daddy left soon afterwards. They were glad to get it over with and to get home.

1978 started a bit better than 1977. Mummy was happy that she had her grandad, brothers and sisters back talking to us again. We often had some of them over visiting us which meant we got to see our cousins. On one occasion when Uncle Paddy was over with two of his children, we were all sitting in the living room watching TV when the Pope just happened to come on the channel that was on. James and Sammy both jumped up and shouted, "Fuck off, ye Fenian bastard." I thought it was funny, but I could see on the faces of Sean and Francis that they didn't like it. They got up and told their daddy they wanted to go home now; Sean whispered to Uncle Paddy what had happened. He made his excuses and left. They didn't come round much after that. James and Sammy got the belt that night and I got a smack on the bum. I did, however, hear Daddy say to Mummy later on that it was no big loss as he didn't like Paddy that much. What he said was, "He's a sneaky bastard and I don't trust him at all. There's just something that niggles me about him." Mummy agreed and said the boys were wrong to do that, but that it was all down to being at the big school. As far as Uncle Paddy goes, I liked him, as did the rest of the boys. The murders in Ulster were still happening and on a larger scale, and the IRA were bombing England more and more. The British Army shot dead three IRA terrorists and a passing UVF man in a case of mistaken identity at a postal depot in Belfast. The UVF for some reason kidnapped a priest but let him go unharmed. The IRA exploded over fifty bombs in towns across Northern Ireland, and the INLA assassinated a Conservative MP and an advisor to Margaret Thatcher. I could go on and on with the atrocities carried out that year. Daddy was showing the strain as yet again another one of his company was killed. This time it was one of his cousins. I didn't know the man but I did get to know his brother in later years. Daddy took it bad and seemed to get a hardened stance on religion. I suppose I would feel the same if it was my friends and family being killed, which I did in later years. More sadness would hit us coming near to the end of 1978. Grandad R passed away of old age. He was a great man and to us children he was a monster of a man, over six-foot-tall and like a brick shithouse. He died in his sleep, which is the way to go. Daddy didn't take it too bad because he was a fair age. He was 85 years old. James took it bad as he was the first male born in the family circle. 1978 had now come and gone with the same old thing. Death on the streets of Ulster and death on the streets of England and guess what, 1979 started the same way. Deaths, deaths and more deaths.

At the beginning of 1979, Daddy had to deal with a large loss of life to the British Army. Eighteen British Army soldiers were killed when the IRA exploded two roadside bombs as a British convoy passed by. He was in the area when it happened so he was in the thick of it. The terrorists were now attacking the heart of government and being very successful at it as well. I was getting ready to go to big school in September to join James and Sammy. One thing Mummy said to me on my first day was, "Don't pick up any bad language when you're there." That was referring to James and Sammy using bad language when Uncle Paddy and his boys were visiting us. It had been quite a while since we saw Uncle Paddy and family round the house so we knew he was upset at what happened, but it was only boys being boys. Daddy was doing well at work, Mummy was happy at home looking after the family and all us boys were growing up in a great environment. Life was good for our family. That all changed very quickly near the end of 1979.

Chapter 3
Daddy's Death

It was a normal Saturday morning and what we always looked forward to—a day off school and staying in bed as long as we wanted. The only thing to do was to do nothing. With so many of us boys in the house, everyone wanted to go to work with Dad. Dad wasn't out on patrol on the Friday night as he went out every other weekend with the UDR. That's the reason he worked his day job this Saturday. This weekend Billy and Sammy got to go. James didn't want to go that much anymore. He got to that age where he just wanted to stay out late and sleep all morning. For us, that was the only reason we would want to get up early: to go to work with Dad. I was in bed reading the Dandy when I heard Mum shout, "Billy, Sammy, your dad says he's going in ten minutes."

Next thing you know, you could hear the rumble of the two of them running down the stairs. Within two minutes, they were dressed and ready to go. Mum would not let any of us leave the house without first having breakfast, and if you did, you would soon hear about it. There's one thing for sure; if mum barked out, you listened. She was never harsh, but if you crossed her, she could bite your head off in seconds. "You're not leaving the house until you have cleared the bowls now, boys. I'm not having you two go about that garage saying you're starving. Your daddy has enough to do without listening to you go on about being hungry. And make sure you two have your old work clothes on and not your good ones now. I'm not having any more of your good bloody clothes being ruined." She was always making sure we were all right, warm enough, fed and clean; mind you we never got back home clean. As soon as we heard Dad ask, "Is my flask ready Rose?" we knew it was time to go. Up got Billy and Sammy, raring to go. "Right, I'll see you later." Like a shot, Billy and Sammy ran like hell to the car. We had a Vauxhall at the time. They soon stopped in their tracks though when Dad shouted, "Check the car, cubs."

There's one thing Dad taught every one of us to do every single time we were going out in the car. We had to check the car for bombs. We all knew what was supposed to be under the car and we also knew what was not supposed to be there, and if we saw something, we knew what to do: calmly get up and tell Dad. It was just in case someone was watching us. We always knew it could happen but because we did it so often it become normal and with no fear. I'm sure if we did find something we would scream and run like hell. We didn't think like that though. One other thing Dad did rely on was that we had a dog in the garden, and if anyone came round the house, the dog let us know. Root was a great gun dog and a great guard dog. I remember lying in bed listening to Root bark like mad. Dad would get up and have a look before telling Root to stop. Now this is just not Dad shouting. He would simply say, "Root, go to bed." Root would hear him, stop right away and go to bed. He was a great dog, trained to the max. He also carried a personal weapon for protection in his holster and was ready at any given time to draw it.

At this point, I would always sit up in bed and look out the window to see them leave. There was always a fight to see who got to sit in the front seat. And no matter the age or size of each other, we would always argue and fight. It always ended with Dad shouting, "Stop it and get in the bloody car or you won't get to go again." That's when the younger brother usually got the front seat because Dad would look at the bigger one with a bit of anger on his face. I remember looking down and Billy was getting into the front seat of the car with a big grin on his face; then, when you looked at Sammy's face he had a look of anger on his. He was the older brother and he had to sit in the back seat. Like clockwork, dad would open the boot, check the inside and put his boiler suit and flask in the boot. He would always be looking around getting into the car. He would always tell us, "These cowardly bastards would only come at you when your back is turned so always keep a look round you, cubs." Cubs is a word he used a lot. If he wanted us to do anything, he would shout, "One of you cubs get some turf for the fire." We heard that a lot.

The car always started on the second or third turn of the key, but if it didn't, we would all be getting out of bed sooner than we wanted. Many times, we heard mum shout: "James, Stephen, get up; your father needs a push start." That would always get James up because if dad was late because he wouldn't get up he would get a beating with the belt. This time the Vauxhall started, so James could snore away.

As I looked down, Billy looked up at me with a look of glee on his face sitting up front. Billy was always one for wanting to be up front with Dad driving. He wasn't the same when Mum was driving. It's just that he wanted to sit up front because Dad would drive faster; Billy had a love for going fast. That never stopped when he got older.

As Dad reversed the car out, the last thing I would have thought was that's the last time I will see him alive. As he put the car in first gear and drove off, he looked back and stuck his thumb up at Mum and drove off. Billy was grinning away like a Cheshire cat and Sammy was in the back, comic in hand.

That was the last time our family would be happy. Over the years, Sammy and Billy would tell us what happened from that point onwards and it never changed. Usually stories would change with bits added or left out. This story never changed. It was word for word every time.

I remember on one occasion in later years, Sammy and myself were having a chat about our lives, the journeys we took from Dad's death to now.

It was on one of those occasions when he told me his account, explaining virtually every second in the car as if he was back in that awful time and to me it felt like I was in the back seat with him.

40

Sammy's Words

I remember Mum shouting: "Billy, Sammy, your dad says he's going in ten minutes." I got up right away and got dressed, ran down stairs to get some breakfast, and as usual, Mummy had tea and toast ready on the table. Both of us got stuck in, eager to get away. Daddy was lacing up his boots and eating at the same time. Both Billy and myself were always trying to show Daddy we were ready to go and waiting on that word. Mummy as usual warned us, "You're not leaving the house until you have cleared the bowls now, boys. I'm not having you two go about that garage saying you're starving. Your daddy has enough to do without listening to you go on about being hungry."

Just as soon as Mummy warned us, Daddy said, "Is my flask ready, Rose?"

That was it; we were off. It was now a race to the car. Billy was on the outside of the table so he got the jump on me. As we ran to the car, we were pushing, shoving each other and laughing at the same time. I remember Daddy shouting at us. Just kids being kids.

"Check the car, cubs." Billy crawled under the passenger side and I did the back. I shouted, 'Nothing,' to Daddy and got out from underneath the car. Billy got there first so he got the front seat. He was a friger and always got there first.

"Do you remember me looking up at you, Stephen?"

"Yes, I do. You made a bloody face at me, you friger." He was laughing at me because he was going, and I wasn't.

"I only did it 'cause Daddy was at the boot." I remember when we started off, I began to read my comic. Dad started to hum along to a song on the radio which didn't mean so much then but now when I hear it, it always brings me back to that Saturday morning in the car. My Sweet Lord, George Harrison. At one point, he started to sing do-do-do along with the guitar part and looked at us when he did. We laughed and eventually joined in.

We turned the corner at the top of the Cross and headed towards Daddy's work. I was busy humming away to the music on the radio and reading the Dandy when Daddy and

Billy started talking about our dog Root barking again last night. I could hear them, but I wasn't really paying much attention. It was about three minutes after we turned the corner that it all started.

We approached a dip in the road before a left-hand bend when what sounded like loud cracking started. It was like someone was throwing loads of stones at the car.

Daddy shouted: "Get down, get down." We turned to the left and the crackling got more and more aggressive. Daddy was still shouting and trying to control the car. That's when I felt a sharp burning sting to my leg. I started screaming, not knowing what was happening to me. Billy was in the front under the dash where Dad shoved him, crying and looking up at Daddy for help and reassurance. I was still screaming when I looked down at my leg and the red blood started soaking through my trousers. Then, it happened again. Yet another sharp burning sensation but this time to my belly. I let a roar out of me which got Daddy's attention. He reached round his seat and grabbed me, shouting, "Are you all right, Sammy? Hang on cubs, it's okay."

As the car swung to the right on the right-hand bend, I could hear the car engine stopping. Daddy started to shout, "You fucking bastards." He leaned out of the broken front window and started firing his hand gun. The cracking stopped hitting the car. Just goes to prove that they don't like it when you shoot back at them. He started roaring like hell at whatever or who was attacking us. At that stage, everything went quiet for what felt like minutes but was only seconds. Billy was still under the dashboard crying, without a sound coming from him, while Daddy was crouched over, forward and to the middle of the car. He was holding onto Billy's hand and kept repeating, "It's okay cubs, it's okay." His voice got weaker and weaker but he never stopped trying to reassure us. I was trying to say Daddy, Daddy, I'm bleeding Daddy. I could hear him trying to say Sammy over and over again. Just as soon as it stopped, it started again but this time short bursts. I could see Daddy being thrown back into the seat. That's when I got hit again in my arm. I passed out at that stage but when I spoke to Billy about what happened after I passed out, I'm glad I didn't see what he had seen.

Billy used to talk a lot about it to me when we were young but when he got to a certain age, he would never, and I mean never, talk about it. He would ignore me and just walk away. Sometimes, he would shout at me telling me to stop it and go away, but when he told me to "fuck off", I knew to let it go and leave him alone. He would run away crying and usually end up outside with Root throwing stones at the tyres of Daddy's big truck. As with my unforgettable memories of that day, I never forgot what Billy told me of his account of the following moments after I passed out.

Billy's Words

The one image I can never blank out was when the last burst of gun fire happened; Daddy was fired back in his seat and I saw a bullet hit him in the chest near his arm.

He was still conscious with his gun in his right hand. He had just unloaded his gun out the front window shouting and swearing at the same time, but that last burst was bad. He kept trying to get you to answer him, Sammy, but you didn't answer back. He kept trying to turn around to see you, but every time he tried, a shot would ring out.

I thought you were dead. All I could see was your legs between the seats. Then he leaned down and grabbed me by the hand; he had blood on his face and it was running out his nose and mouth. He was trying to say something to me but I couldn't make him out. He had blood in his mouth. It sounded like, "You're all right cub, they have gone, don't worry anymore."

Then it happened. Out of the silence appeared a man with a balaclava on and pointing a hand gun at the car. He walked up to Daddy's door where the glass was gone, smashed by the hail of bullets. It all seemed to happen in slow motion, which is why I will never forget it. He looked at Daddy through the cut-out eyes of his mask with a look of a monster about to kill his prey. He started to grin at Daddy as he lifted his arm, and as it rose, I could see his murderous weapon appear, ready to take another innocent life. He stopped level with his head and pointed the gun, he then smiled at him and shouted, "*Chuckie ar la*," which is supposed to mean 'our day will come'. Daddy never took his eyes off me or turned to make eye contact with the gunman. I suppose he knew what was coming and didn't want to give the bastard the satisfaction of seeing the fear in his eyes which is what some murderers need to see before they take a life. Not until the end did Daddy take his eyes off of me. He tried smiling but before he could, the bullet ripped through his head. He fell forward with his head coming to rest on my seat. All I could focus on was Daddy's eyes staring in my direction but lifeless; I was covered in blood and lumps of Daddy's hair and skin all over me. Again, it felt like it was all in slow motion. Before the gunman lowered his gun, he looked at me with a grin and with a look in his eyes. It was a look of pure evil. It is the closest I will ever want to be to the devil's ways and that's what this was. A look I will never ever forget and eyes I will never ever forget. That grin on his face will live with me for ever. Before he made his escape, he leaned into the car and took Daddy's gun from his bloodied hand. "I'll have that, thank you very much." Then he simply just walked away. I could hear him roar with laughter as he walked away. It's only then did I find out there was more than one gunman. They all joined in with the laughter as they left. I didn't find out until later in life that there were four of them involved in the shooting. They must have been watching Daddy's movements for a long time because they knew where and when to attack. They hit the car at a point where they had three points of attack. The first attack happened as we approached a dip in the road. There are two bends after the dip which starts with a left hand bend and then to the right before a straight. Daddy made it to the second turn which was a right. That's when the car mounted the hedge and came to a standstill.

There was a gunman as we approached the first bend, another as we turned left, then one more as we turned to the right. They had it all planned out and as we now know, it wasn't the first or last time they would use such tactics to kill someone. I was still crouching under the dash holding on to Daddy's hand. I kept saying in a soft broken voice, "Daddy, Daddy, Daddy wake up Daddy, please Daddy." But nothing came from him. I just kept waiting and hoping that he would answer me. I felt something run down my hand and as I looked, I had a puddle of blood in the palm of my hand. It was running down Daddy's arm and coming to an end in my palm.

Everything was so quiet, I could hear the cows in the fields and birds singing away. It seemed like the world was just getting on with living, not caring what had just happened to us. I was on my own. Daddy and Sammy both would not answer me. I kept shouting and shouting at them but they did not answer.

All I could do was cry and cry and hope they would answer me. It felt like hours that I was alone. I kept holding on to Daddy's hand waiting for him to move and say something. That never happened. All of a sudden, I heard a car coming down the road at a fast speed. Brakes screeched and someone started to scream, "No, no, no, God no. William, William." I looked up and I could see Uncle Sam and Aunty June.

Uncle Sam kept saying, "William, can you hear me William?" He didn't answer.

Then, Aunty June started scream. "O God, Sam, SAM? Sammy's in the back; he's been shot. O God please no no. Sammy, can you hear me?"

Uncle Sam shouted at June, "Go for help, June, quickly." I could hear her run to a local house screaming as she ran. Uncle Sam kept saying, "Can you hear me, Sammy? Can you hear me lad?" I was still under the dash but this time very quiet, still hand in hand with Daddy. I would not let go of him because I thought if I let go he would not wake up and he would be gone for ever. Uncle Sam looked at me and shouted, "You all right, Billy, are you hit, boy? Billy, are you hit?" I could not answer. I was in shock.

Aunty June arrived back and Uncle Sam shouted, "Help Billy, June, he's in the front. I can't get him to answer me."

She opened the door on my side of the car and very slowly and gently reached in. I could hear her talking to me but it was just a noise with no meaning. I just kept looking at Daddy and holding his hand. She gently reached over, touched Daddy's hand to feel for a pulse. She then turned my head towards her and started speaking. Again, I had no idea what she was saying. She reached over to my hand that was holding Daddy's hand and tried to release it. I was holding on for dear life. "Let go, Billy. Let go of your daddy, pet. Uncle Sam needs to help him". When she said that I let go. She then lifted me out from underneath the dash and sat me on the seat. Only then did I start to understand her. "Billy, can you hear me darling?" She checked me over for injuries before lifting me out of the car and taking me to her car. She sat me in the front seat and put her coat around me. "I'll be back in a moment, Billy; I'm just going to help Sammy." As I sat in that car, I felt like I was alone, invisible and in a nightmare of which I had no control. I looked down at all the blood on my clothes and on my skin. Then a drip of blood dripped off my eyebrow on to my cheek. I lifted my hand to rub it off and when I looked in my hand there was an awful lot of blood in my palm. My hand was covered in Daddy's blood. I looked at it with fear. I tried in vain to rub it off like a disease but it wouldn't come off. I rubbed and rubbed at it. I started to panic. My breathing got heavier until I started to cry. No one came to help me. Little did I know that no one could hear me cry because of all the commotion and activity around helping Sammy and Daddy.

People started to arrive from local houses and vehicles that were on the road. One lady who stopped at Uncle Sam's car just happened to look in at me in the car crying. She knew I was in a bad way. She opened the door and leaned in to help me. She started to wipe my face of all the blood on me. She was crying and praying to God. I could tell that this lady was a Catholic because she kept crossing herself. She kept kissing me on the forehead and asking God, "Why would you let this happen, God? Poor wee lad's done no harm." When she wiped the blood from my arms, she uncovered cuts from the glass but luckily no bullet wounds. She wiped the blood from the palm of my hands which to me removed that fear and disease I had. At that point, I didn't know what to do or think. I was looking over at Daddy; he was so still and motionless. Uncle Sam eventually put a coat over him to stop people gawking at him.

After that, I remember looking at Sammy. He was moving but I knew it didn't look good. All of a sudden, I could hear the sound of sirens. The noise was getting louder and louder and before long the noise stopped and policemen were everywhere. What took me out of the shock I was in was the noise of a large chinook helicopter landing in the field next to us. The cows and birds I heard after the shooting suddenly stopped. The birds disappeared and all the cows ran away. That quite sombre moment that I will never forget turned to rage and anger. That rage and anger is something I will never want to remember. Screams, shouting, anger and frustration was everywhere.

I heard a scream that made me jump and when I looked in that direction, it was Aunty June who was helping Sammy.

"He's not breathing, Sam, where the hell is the ambulance?" A lady from a local house started to give him CPR and June gave him mouth to mouth until a medic that was on the helicopter arrived on the scene. Compared to everyone else, he was calm and in full control of the situation. Within minutes, I could hear another siren. This time it was an ambulance. They got to work on Sammy right away and before you knew it, he was put on the stretcher and on his way to the back of the ambulance. I started crying and began to shout his name. One of the medics came over to me to check me out. "Okay, let's get him in the ambulance with the first lad."

Uncle Sam come over to me and said, "He's going to be all right Billy, you look after him for me now, okay. I will follow you down the road." Before I knew it, that siren noise was louder than ever before and went on and on. It didn't dawn on me that it was because we were inside the ambulance. The rest of that day after we reached the county hospital is a mishmash of memories. They give me a sedative to calm me down. I don't even remember Mummy arriving at the hospital.

This is always where Billy stopped talking about his recollection and memories of that day's events. He could never get away from the awful things he'd seen. It seemed that when the madness of that day on the road outside the Cross ended and he headed off in the ambulance, his recollection of events ended. The moment my life changed for ever. It happened at 9.15 am on Saturday the 10th December 1979, two weeks before Christmas.

I was still in bed with my comic when a loud vehicle pulled up outside the house. When I sat up in bed and looked out the same window I did when Daddy left for work, it turned out to be two police land rovers and Uncle Jimmy and Aunty Diane in their car.

They looked angry for some reason. Jimmy and Diane walked round the back of the house. That's where people always come into our house. I could hear voices downstairs but couldn't make them out, so as every child does I got up and went to the top of the stairs and put my head through the banisters. Within seconds of getting there, Mummy started screaming, "No, no, oh please God, no." To hear Mummy crying the way she did. I knew something bad had happened. James came bursting out his bedroom door and said what is wrong with Mummy.

"Don't know but she's crying, and Uncle Jimmy and Aunty Diane are down there. There's loads of police out the front as well." We both raced down the stairs and into the kitchen. As we opened the door, we could see that Mummy was crawled up in a ball in the corner with Boyd in her arms, who was only a baby at that time, crying her eyes out.

We were both so scared and didn't know what was going on. Uncle Jimmy made his way over to us and said, "Come on into the living room, cubs, come on. Diane, you stay with Rose." He walked us out of the kitchen, into the living room where John was sitting on the floor playing. He was only 3 years old at the time. I remember him looking up at me and smiling as he always did thinking we were going to play with him. He told us to sit down beside him.

"Now listen, cubs. I have some bad news to tell you and I want you to be brave, okay. Your mummy is going to need you cubs to help her out now, especially you, James; you're the oldest." We were so scared at this point.

I asked, "What's wrong with Mummy, Uncle Jimmy?" The next words to come out of his mouth was that moment— the moment that changed my life for ever.

"Your daddy's just been shot on the way to work." At this moment, his voice changed. He put his arms around us both and said, "Your daddy's dead, boys. He's gone."

Fear is a word that takes many forms. Fear of heights, fear of spiders etc. This form of fear is something that you can never explain or understand. I felt sick, scared and cold. I started to shake uncontrollably. My mouth became dry and my eyes became blinded with tears. I tried to get up, but Jimmy wouldn't let me. I started to struggle with him, but he just kept me tight to his side with his arms around me. James was still and unresponsive. His face was grey and his hands, well, it's hard to explain. His palms were upright, and his fingers were making shapes as if he was doing a puzzle while his lips were moving as if to talk. Uncle Jimmy just kept saying it's okay boys, it's okay. What felt like hours was just moments, we just sat there with Uncle Jimmy holding us and trying to keep us calm. All of a sudden, James spoke. It was so quiet and soft, Uncle Jimmy had to ask twice.

"What happened to Daddy? Why is he dead?" I looked up at Uncle Jimmy for answers to why he said Daddy was dead.

"Do you know when your daddy gets you all to check the car every time you get into it? Well, it's because there are bad men out there who want to harm him and anyone like him. Well, those bad men shot your daddy on the way to his work and he died."

Both I and James just sat there in complete disbelief for a while. All of a sudden, I started to shake uncontrollably and before long I was crying uncontrollably. Soon James started to cry but he was still somewhat quiet and was crying within.

I looked down at John sitting on the floor who just didn't know what to think of us and he started to cry, but it was because of the noise around him and not necessarily about Daddy's death.

We could still hear Mummy in the kitchen screaming, crying and shouting. She would not accept what Aunty Diane and the police officer were saying.

All of a sudden, we heard Mummy shout, "Sammy and Billy. Where's Sammy and Billy? Tell me where they are. Sweet Jesus not the boys as well. Please no, not them too. NO, NO, NO, NO, NO."

I looked at James, then we both looked at Uncle Jimmy. We both just started screaming and crying at him. I began to hit him wanting him to tell me that they were okay. "They are all right lads; they are okay. Sammy's been hurt but listen to me boys, he's going to be okay, and Billy's fine. He's just got a few cuts and bruises, that's all. I should think he'd be home later today." It didn't stop us crying though. Then the moment that calmed us down a bit happened. Mummy, with Boyd in her arms, rushed out of the kitchen and into the living room where we were. We both rushed over to her as she appeared in the doorway. "Come here, boys, come here. You're okay now, you're okay." She asked James to pick up John and bring him over.

"Mummy, Uncle Jimmy said Daddy's dead, is he Mummy?" She didn't answer at first; she just kept stroking our cheeks and foreheads as if to wipe the hair from our eyes. She just kept repeating it's okay it's okay. At that point, Aunty Diane stood in the doorway. I looked at her and she give me a loving smile before putting her hand on her mouth. I could see the tears welling in her eyes as she tried to be strong in front of us. Mummy then began to tell us what had happened. "I don't want any of this to be true, boys. I want it to be a big fat lie, but," she hesitated for a second and tried again, "but it's not. Your daddy's been killed. He's been shot dead. He's gone. Gone, gone, gone." Every single person in that room, including the RUC man standing with Uncle Jimmy, was crying. The image of Mummy with four young children telling them such horrid news about their daddy would have upset even the hardest of men.

Then they all left the room leaving Mummy and us boys alone to try and take in what we had just been told. We just cried and cried and hugged each other. Poor John and Boyd were at an age where they didn't know what was going on. John was crying because we were crying and Boyd, still a baby in Mummy's arms, just looked at us.

After about ten minutes, Mummy said, "We need to get up, boys, there's a lot to do now." She handed Boyd to James and asked me to take care of John. "Now I need you older boys to take care of the babies while I go into the kitchen. Stay here and be good for me, will you?" She kissed every one of us on the forehead and left the room. I went over to the large window only to see what looked like hundreds of UDR and RUC men walking around the front of the house. They looked at me in the window and just looked away. It was like they didn't want to look at us because they were angry at what happened to Daddy. Uncle Jimmy walked past and tapped the window and winked at me before walking up to a UDR man and shook his hand. They started to talk and turned their backs on us. Another helicopter landed in the field, out of my view, at the side of the house. I can only assume that more soldiers got out of it. Round about ten minutes later, Uncle Sam and Aunty June arrived and went directly over to Uncle Jimmy. They hugged each other like only real hard men do. I didn't know at that point that Uncle Sam arrived on the scene just after the shooting. Aunty June went directly round the back of the house to see Mummy. Aunty June come into the room soon after and gave us all a hug. She reached into her pocket and pulled out some sweets before sharing them with us. James asked her before she sat down, "Where're Sammy and Billy? Are they going to die as well?" Even though we had already been told that they would be okay, we just kept asking everybody the same question. It's as if we needed to hear it over and over again to make sure it was true.

Aunty June, in a raised voice, said, "No, of course they are not. Sammy's not well in hospital but he's going to be okay. They are operating on him now, but he will be all right. Billy's fine. He's got cuts and bruises, but he could be home soon." John was a lot happier by now and content eating his sweets while sitting on Aunty June's lap. Boyd was sleeping on the settee. She did calm us down a lot, but then she was always very kind to us and we liked her. She stayed with us until Mummy come back into the room. She sat down beside us and said, "Listen, boys. I have to go down to the County Hospital to see Sammy and Billy. Now, I want you to be good while I'm away and look after John and Boyd. I am relying on you two to be good until I'm back." Aunty June then said, "Don't you worry, Rose; get down to the County Hospital and see how the cubs are. I'm sure they need their mummy too. I will look after the boys until you're back."

Mummy got up and left without saying anything. I could hear her say to Uncle Sam, "Can we go, Sam?" Uncle Sam come into the room and hugged us all before giving Aunty June a kiss. He told us all to be good and that he would be back soon.

The rest of that day was so mad. There were people coming and going everywhere. Some we knew and some we didn't. They just kept coming. Lots of UDR and RUC men at every turn. We passed the time watching cartoons on TV or whatever was on. It was just background stuff. Aunty June called us to the table for something to eat. It was 4 p.m. and we hadn't eaten since our breakfast around 9 a.m. so we were hungry. As we sat at the table eating, I could hear lots of noise upstairs in the back room.

I asked Aunty June what it was, and she said, "Don't worry, eat up like a good cub." Little did we know that someone was clearing the back room so that Daddy's coffin could go in there. We finished off eating and I asked if it was okay to go to the toilet. As I went up the stairs, I looked into the back room and Uncle Jimmy and Aunty Diane were taking the bed apart. I met another man coming out of Mummy and Daddy's bedroom. He put his hand on my head and asked me if I was okay. I ran down the stairs and whispered to James what I'd seen. He knew right away what they were doing and told me. "That's where Daddy's coffin will be."

Around about 6 p.m. I heard Mummy's voice. We were back in the living room and didn't see her arrive back because of the dark evening. She came in to see us as soon as she arrived. She looked so tired and her eyes were red from all the obvious crying she had done. She sat us down and explained to us how Sammy and Billy were. "Sammy has had an operation on some wounds. He was shot, but don't be getting upset because he's going to be okay. Billy is fine. He only has some bad cuts to his arms and face. He's okay and he will be home tomorrow so don't be worrying about them. They are in great hands now. I have to go and get your daddy and bring him home. He's at the morgue, but June will be staying with you until we get back, okay! Now I'm going upstairs to get changed." I then interrupted by saying, "Mummy, they have taken the beds out of the back room. Where are we going to sleep?"

"Don't worry," she said, "we will all sleep in the same room together tonight." She kissed us all before leaving us to get Daddy.

I wasn't prepared for what was about to happen next.

Chapter 4
Daddy Comes Home

We sat in the living room in the middle of so many people: ladies coming and going with tea, coffee and plates and plates of sandwiches and buns. They would always ask us if we needed anything to eat. Both James and I always went for the cream buns. I just knew I would end up being as sick as a dog but who cares, it's free cream buns. I turned to James and asked him, "Where's Mummy? What's keeping her?" He told me to be quiet; she wouldn't be long. As soon as the words came out of his mouth, we heard cars pulling up outside and all the people sitting with us put their cups down and started going outside. Another one of Daddy's brothers, Uncle George, came in to the room and asked me and James to come out the back. I put my bun on the coffee table and left with him right away. He walked us through the kitchen and out the back door towards the front of the house where there were hundreds and hundreds of people. There were so many men in uniform, both army and police. Uncle George walked us through the crowd of people asking so many times to excuse him as he took us through.

We eventually got to the front drive and the car park where there was a large space where UDR men lined up on both sides. It wasn't long before the sergeant standing at the front shouted out, "Company"; it sounded like someone switched the sound off. Everything went quiet. "Company attention." The sound of so many boots standing to attention in the dead of night was something to hear and see. Not a word, not a sound and not a movement was to be heard in the car park. To my right, I could see a dark vehicle reversing into the space the soldiers made beforehand. Then I realised what was happening. It was the hearse with Daddy inside.

I had a feeling inside me right away. It was fear. All of a sudden, I was so scared. I came to a halt just as it approached the first soldier. The sergeant then shouted out, "Guard of honour, attention." Again, the boots standing to attention cut through the night air.

"Bye the left slow march." They slow marched their way to the back of the hearse where the back door was open. "Company attention." I could feel Uncle George grasp my hand so very tight as the soldiers turned inwards to face each other. Then, Mummy appeared from the front of the hearse. My heart seemed to miss a beat. She made her way and stood at the back of the hearse in front of the coffin. She looked so alone and sad which made me cry just to see her like that. She leaned forward and laid her hand on top of the Union Jack covered coffin. At that point, our minister, the Reverend Brown, who was behind Mummy, asked everyone to bow their heads in prayer. I remember everyone in one voice saying the Lord's Prayer. When Reverend Brown said amen, Mummy moved to the side. The six UDR men then started to take Daddy's coffin out of the hearse. Tears started to flow from every person there, but one thing that I could hear was poor Root, Daddy's dog, who started to whine at the side of the house. Did he know? I kept thinking about what was going on. This was all so surreal. Just hours ago, I was looking out the bedroom window at Daddy, Sammy and Billy leaving for work. Now, he was coming home in a coffin. They lifted Daddy high and began the last march. For Daddy, this would be the last time he came home to us. James was standing to my left holding onto Uncle George's hand, and he looked so lost. Next thing I know he lets go and runs to Mummy. She opens her arms and welcomes him with a big hug. I could see her ask where I was. He pointed towards us. She told Uncle George to bring me over. I got one of those hugs as well. She stood up tall with James on one side and me on the other. We walked behind the UDR men, carrying Daddy's coffin towards the front door of the house. So many people, young and old, men and women who wanted to touch the coffin and say their bit. They would touch it and say, "God bless William." It just showed how much Daddy was thought of in the Cross. As soon as they got the coffin inside, they took it straight upstairs into the back room where I saw them working earlier in the day. Mummy took us into the kitchen and sat us down beside the stove. She knelt down to us. "Listen boys, do you want to go up and see your daddy? There's nothing to worry about now, he just looks like he's sleeping, and it's okay if you don't want to." I looked at James and we both nodded our heads yes.

"Okay, now just take it easy and hold on to me. I want you both to be brave and remember it's your daddy and he would never hurt you." As we went up the stairs, the UDR men who had just carried Daddy upstairs moved to the side for us to get through. As we got to the door, I could see Reverend Brown waiting for us. He started to pray as we entered the room and there at the back of the room with two UDR men on each side was Daddy's coffin. Mummy walked over to us and asked us if we were ready and if we were okay. In a very weak voice, I muttered, "Uh-huh." James never spoke.

"Here we go," Mummy said. We walked towards the back of the room getting closer and closer but at the same time getting more scared. Mummy stopped at the bottom of the coffin and let go of our hands. She walked over to the top of the coffin, leaned in and kissed Daddy's forehead. That's when James turned and ran out of the room, crying as he went. Reverend Brown went after him but Mummy said, "It's okay, let him be for now." Mum called me to her side to see Daddy. I walked round to the top on the same side of Mummy and reached for her hand. She grabbed it so tightly and that kind of helped me. "There's your daddy, home again." I looked up to see my daddy in a coffin, he looked asleep and seemed to be at peace.

"He looks asleep, Mummy," I said.

"I only wish he was, pet," Mummy said. She started to talk to him as if he was alive and okay and about to wake up. She kissed him again, then looked at me and asked me if I wanted to kiss him before we went downstairs. Again I muttered, "Uh-huh". She helped me up, and I leaned in and kissed him on the forehead just like Mummy did. "Good boy; right, let's go downstairs for now; there's a lot of people want to come up and pay their respects to William." As we left the room, I looked back, hoping to see Daddy looking back at me. It was a false hope. We made our way past so many people to get to the kitchen where James was in Granny R's arms, crying his heart out. Mummy went over and gave him a hug which helped him and calmed him down a bit. The house was full of Mummy and Daddy's brothers and sisters. Every one of them took their turn to hug Mummy and come over to bless me and James. I looked over to see John and Boyd still being looked after by Aunty June and Aunty Diane. They looked content. All night long they carried tea and coffee to the people inside and outside. There was an endless supply of trays full of sandwiches and buns. Everywhere you looked in the kitchen were teabags, sugar, coffee, milk and, of course, cream cakes. On days like this, the community, both Catholic and Protestant, pull together to help the affected family. So many people called to help Mummy in her hour of need. Mummy's brothers and sisters who were Catholic were doing all they could to help out. The religious divide did not matter tonight. There was one person who walked into the house and stopped everybody in their tracks as he passed by. He darkened the room with his vast size, blocking out the light wherever he went. I met this man a couple of times before at a local Sunday school event in the Cross. You could never mistake the man wherever he went. It was the Reverend Ian Paisley. He preached his first ever sermon in the Cross and he had family ties to the Cross area. He walked up to Mummy after being introduced to her by Uncle Sam.

He leaned over her and whispered something to her. She looked at him before getting up off her seat. He put his arms around her like an old friend before making their way upstairs to see Daddy. They spent quite some time upstairs talking to different people about the shooting. Sometime later, the big man appeared in the kitchen again. He walked towards us and immediately got down on his knees to talk to us. "I'm so sorry for the loss of your father, children. I will pray for all of you in this, your time of need, and remember, God will make sure the evil murderers who carried out this horrendous, barbaric act will meet their maker at the altar of God. I will pray that you can and will be strong for your mother and for each other. God will bless you." With that, he got up, walked outside to where the masses of people congregated and asked everyone to pray with him. His voice carried across the park and you would have to be deaf not to hear him. It's not the first time we heard him pray. He spent most of the night talking to people who visited the house and from what people said, he stayed until past midnight. There was a lot of anger about Daddy's death directed at him, but he would be used to that as he probably had a funeral to go to every week and sometimes two or three.

I was getting so tired by now. It was nearly 12 midnight and the house was still so busy with people. I wanted to go to bed; I was so tired. I found Mummy with Aunty June in the living room talking away and she looked so tired and so sad. I walked up to her and gave her a big hug. "Hello, pet. Thank you, Stephen. You okay?" She introduced me to some people with her who started saying I was cute. I whispered to Mummy that I was tired and wanted to go to bed. I didn't know where I was to sleep because John and Boyd were in my bed because of Daddy being in their bedroom. "I'm not surprised. You have been so good today helping out with the children. Come with me. I'll be back in a minute, June." She opened the door quietly so as not to wake Boyd or John and told me to get into bed with John. "James can sleep in my bed tonight." She tucked me in and told me I was a brave boy today. She kissed me and said goodnight. I gave her a big hug and said goodnight back to her. I lay my head on the pillow and within seconds, fell asleep.

The next day I awoke with Boyd all over me looking to play. For a few moments, I forgot what happened the day before and everything seemed fine, just like a normal Sunday morning. Then, the reality hit me. I got up and sneaked open the door to find Uncle Billy at the door of the back room. He looked round and said, "Hello cub, you're up then." Uncle Alan was a heavy drinker and no doubt he was still drunk from after the night before. That's why I didn't see him around. He was always the joker and would always make us laugh. His party trick was to ride a bicycle while sitting on the handle bars facing backwards. He lifted me up for a hug and told me I was getting heavier before letting me down again. I could smell the drink on him. I took Boyd by the hand and we both went downstairs. Yet again, the house was still busy with people were helping Mummy out. Before we knew it, we were at the table having breakfast. James and John were already there sitting beside some of our cousins. Soon they got up and went outside. As they left, Mummy come in the back door and said hi to us. She said, "I have some good news, boys. I'm going to pick up Billy from the County. He's well enough to come home." I asked if I could go with her, but she said she wanted me to help out taking care of John and Boyd. "I will be back before you know it, darling." She got her coat and left with Aunty Sally, who was married to Uncle George.

I would go on to spend some of my best summers with Aunty Sally's family in the countryside. I loved every moment I spent there. Aunty Sally had a brother not much older than me. We were so excited that Billy was coming home, but Sammy was still very ill in hospital. We didn't know the true story of how he was. I spent most of the morning with Boyd and John which helped because time went quick. Before we knew it, Mum was back from the hospital with Billy. He seemed to be okay but looked upset with all the UDR and RUC men still roaming around the house. Mum took him straight upstairs where we all joined them. "Don't come too close boys, remember he has some cuts and bruises." I could see some cuts on his forehead and he had stitches on the side of his head. His arms were bandaged up quite a lot. All we wanted to do was ask Billy what happened but for some reason I don't think he would want to talk about it so we just let him be to rest, as he looked so tired. Mummy took us to the side and made us promise not to keep asking him what happened in the car. "He's unwell and still very sad about your daddy, boys, so just give him time and let him sleep. He's had a hard time, so he has."

That's just what we did. We left the room and let him sleep. Just as we were leaving, he screamed at Mummy, "Don't leave, Mummy, come back please." Mummy stopped and told us to go on downstairs. She stayed with Billy until he fell asleep. I can't imagine what was going on in his head having witnessed what he did. We spent the rest of that night being introduced to nearly everyone who called—lots of cousins we haven't seen in ages and Uncles and Aunties we forgot existed. There was, however, one person who was missing up till then and never made an appearance the whole time: Mummy's mother, Granny D as we called her. She never really spoke to us boys and we always knew why. We were Protestants and she was a Catholic. Simple as that. I remember, as a boy, meeting her on the path in the Cross, and when she looked at me, she crossed the road so she didn't have to speak to me. That occurred a lot. That happened to all of us. We never got any birthday or Christmas cards, let alone a present from her. That was just the way it was. Some of our uncles and aunties were the same but not all. Some of Mummy's brothers and sisters were great with us and always came around for visits. Some of Mummy's sisters married Protestant men as well. They, I'm sure, were in the same boat as Mummy. Uncle Paddy and Aunty Ruth seemed to always be around and were helping out a lot today. Uncle Paddy was a funny man who always had a sweet in his pocket for you.

Around about 10 p.m., Uncle Trevor, Daddy's brother, came into the kitchen where Mummy and I were sitting. He whispered that someone was at the back of the house wanting to speak to her. "Who is it, Trevor?" From the look on her face when he told her, it could have been the Queen herself. She got up and stood still for a while before making her way outside. The door was closed behind her as she left.

I asked Aunty Sarah, Uncle Trevor's wife, who it was. "No one you would know Stephen." It turned out to be a local UVF man who wanted to know if there was anything we needed, and if there was, all we had to do is ask. She thanked him but said she would not be asking for help from a group that kill people. Mummy did not take to seeing such a man come to our door and offer his help kindly. She saw the UVF in the same way as the IRA men who killed Daddy. They were both terrorising the communities that we lived in. Of course, others at the house that night would have a different view because of what just occurred. Daddy was from a very large and strong loyalist family circle. As Mummy came back inside, Trevor was still talking to the man outside and he seemed to be quite aggressive towards him. I don't know what was said but the UVF man left right away.

As Uncle Trevor came back, in he went straight to Mummy and said, "Well done, Rose, well done." Things calmed down again after that and it returned to meeting and greeting people that came to pay their respects. A while later, Mummy leaned over and said it was time for bed as we had a big day tomorrow.

"Get the rest of the boys and get up to bed, Stephen. I will be up in a minute to say good night." As I left the room, she told me to tell Billy to get into her bed tonight. I went around the house getting Boyd, John, Billy and James. They all, except James, made their way to bed. James was outside with his friends and said he would be in later. We all went up to bed. On the way up, everyone said good night to us that was in the house. Uncle Paddy was standing outside the back room and sneaked a sweet to every one of us. "Night, cubs, see you all tomorrow." We all said good night back and went to bed. Mummy came up not long after and tucked us all in. She sat on the side of the bed looking so tired. "Tomorrow is going to be a long day for us all and I need you boys to be strong for me. I will be relying on you to help me through. I want to make your daddy up in heaven proud of us all. He will be with us in spirit helping you get through the day." Even though that made us smile a little, seeing Mummy wipe away her tears as she told us made us sad for her. She hugged us all and wished us good night, then left the room.

61

She went to Billy, who was in her bed and I could hear her saying the same to him. I remember thinking after what she had just said Daddy was watching us, and we would be okay. It wasn't long before James came into the room and got into bed with us. We didn't say much that night. We just fell asleep. Tomorrow would come soon enough.

Chapter 5
Saying Goodbye to Daddy

"Stephen, Stephen, wake up, Stephen." That's how the longest day of my life started. It was James, getting us up to get ready for Daddy's funeral. At the bottom of the bed, our suits appeared through the night. No doubt Mummy was up late ironing all our clothes for the day. She would want to make sure that we all looked respectable at the funeral. There were going to be a lot of eyes on us and everyone would be talking about us. We helped John get dressed before dressing ourselves. James was already dressed, apart from his tie. None of us knew how to do one. Daddy would always do our ties for us. I was just about finished when Mummy walked in with Boyd who was already dressed. He looked so happy but then the poor little bugger didn't really know what was ahead of us that day.

"Where's Billy, Mummy?" I asked.

"He's in my room, already dressed." Moments later, he walked into our room; he had a sling on his left arm. By looking in his bloodshot eyes, we could tell he'd been crying all night. Mummy did up our ties one by one just like Daddy used to do. "You will have to learn how to do this yourselves from now on." When we were done, we all made our way downstairs and thanked God the house was empty and quiet. Mummy asked us all to sit at the table for breakfast. "Now for God's sake don't get anything on your clothes. I don't have the time to clean them up." Mummy put Boyd in his chair, then helped Billy. She sat down beside him and helped him with his breakfast. "Now boys listen, I want you all to be strong today and do your best for your daddy. There will be a lot of people here today and I don't want people talking about my boys looking scruffy." She went so quiet all of a sudden and tried to choke back the tears. She knew that today was going to be so hard for us all. She tried to get the words out, but every time she tried, she choked up. Billy reached over and grabbed her hand and for the first time in days had a little smile on his face. She raised her head to him and got the strength to speak. "Now your daddy will be expecting us all to stand proud and not let him down. I know you boys will do just that. We have to keep Sammy in our thoughts as well. He's not well enough yet. Now I know we don't normally do this but I want you all to help me pray for strength today." We said the Lord's Prayer and Mummy asked for the strength to get through the day.

It was just after 11 a.m. when the first knock at the door happened. It was Daddy's brothers and sisters and Granny R. Within minutes, the sandwiches, cakes, tea and coffee were on the go. More and more family members arrived until the house was alive with people but as silent as an empty church at night. I walked outside and could not believe what I was seeing. Thousands upon thousands of people gathered outside the house, in the garden, on the lane and down the drive. Everywhere we looked and as far as the eye could see, people standing in near total silence waiting for the funeral procession to make the journey to the church. Lots of soldiers and policemen all dressed up in their military dressing. I walked through them looking up at them. I was only about four feet tall. The talk was very sombre and not many looked in the mood for a funeral.

It was like I was stuck in a maze of people no matter if I turned left or right. I found myself up beside Root who was tied up outside the garage at the side of the house. I sat with him for a while petting him, but I couldn't get him to respond. He looked as sad as Mummy did this morning. It seemed like I was there for quite some time but before long I could hear Mummy asking if anyone had seen me. I made my way in to see what she wanted. As I walked in the back door she looked at me and grabbed me by the arm. "Look at the shape of you,

Stephen. You're covered in dog hair. What did I tell you about keeping clean?"

Aunty Mary, Mummy's sister, came over and said, "Don't worry, Rose, I'll clean him up. Come on, pet." She took us up to the bathroom to clean me up.

"Why is Mummy mad at me, Aunty Mary?"

"She's not, darling, she's just not coping too well at the moment. There you go, all clean again, my wee love."

We made our way through the people back to the kitchen where Mummy was. "I'm sorry, Mummy. I only wanted to see that Root was okay. He was sad, so I petted him."

She reached down to me and gave me a big hug. "I'm sorry, Stephen, you look lovely again. All handsome and grown up in your gorgeous suit". I started to cry because I felt I let her and Daddy down. I looked around and mostly everyone in the room was crying with me. Aunty Mary knelt down and wiped the tears off my face. "I'll take him outside for a while, Rose, just to calm him down. Come on, pet, let's go and see who's outside." We walked out through the back door and I could see some of my friends from the park and school. Sam called out to me to come over, which I did. Aunty Mary asked me if I was all right now and I said yes.

"Away you go then, pet."

"Thank you, Aunty Mary." Sam, myself and two of our friends from school made our way to the playing field. We just sat and talked about Daddy's death. It was good to get away from the last two days of hell. I even got to laugh a bit. It wasn't long before James came down to get me as it was time to go to the church. As we made our way back to the house, a man stopped us at the edge of the play park. I recognised him from the day before as the man who wanted to speak to Mummy outside the house. "How you all doing, boys. Are you holding up? My name's Jimmy and I'm a cousin of your daddy's. I'm so sorry about your daddy's death, cub. He was a great man who was always very kind to me and helped me out a lot over the years. But now listen, if you boy's ever need anything or any help with someone who is getting to you, make sure you get in touch with me and I will help you out the best I can. It's the least I can do for your daddy. Just ask your Uncle Alan to get in touch with Jimmy Wright for you. He will know what to do". He shook our hands and went back up to the house. As we got back up to the front of the house I could see the UDR men all lined up getting ready to take Daddy to the church. James took me by the hand and led me into a quiet house. Everyone but family was now outside giving us time to say goodbye to Daddy. In the hallway, Billy, John and Boyd were standing waiting for Mummy. She wanted to say goodbye on her own first. We waited and waited until Mummy appeared at the top of the stairs and asked us all to come up. James led the way with me at the end. The five of us got to the top where Mummy asked us if we were ready to say goodbye to Daddy. Not one of us spoke. We all just shook our heads yes. She picked up Boyd and led us into the back room where Daddy was. We walked up and stood around the coffin, looking at Daddy for the last time. "We are all here now, William. I want you to know that we will never let you down and we will all do our best to make you proud of us, and I can promise that we will never, ever give up on finding out who did this to you. Never William, never." The look on Mummy's face, and the way she made that promise to Daddy in his coffin was so strong and powerful. She was so strong. Mummy then asked us all to put our hands on Daddy's heart. We all leaned forward doing so, thinking she was going to say a prayer. You could say it was the complete opposite. She made us promise that we would never give up on Daddy and that we would do whatever it took to get his revenge. She looked at every one of us in turn and waited for us to acknowledge what she had said. We all again nodded our heads yes. She kissed Daddy on the forehead one last time and told him, "That's from wee Sammy William, he's going to be alright. Okay boys, time to give your daddy a kiss goodbye." We all leaned into the coffin one by one and kissed Daddy for the last time.

As Billy did, he whispered "Bye bye, Daddy. I promise, Daddy." After Mummy leaned Boyd into kiss Daddy, she placed a photo of us all on his chest. "Don't forget us in heaven, William, and come to us in our dreams." We all stood back and watched the two soldiers put the lid on the coffin. Hand in hand, as a family, we all cried as one. I looked at Mummy and she was fixated on Daddy as he disappeared from us forever. We would never see him again. Uncle Jimmy came in and give us all a hug. "Okay boys, let's let the soldiers get your daddy downstairs. We all made our way down the stairs and outside where there was a guard of honour on each side. The sergeant brought them to attention for us to walk past. When we passed, he brought them back to stand-at-ease. We all stopped beside the hearse waiting for them to bring Daddy down. I remember Uncle Paddy coming up to us all and telling us to be strong boys for our Daddy before giving us each a sweet and telling us to keep it for the church. It was so quiet with so many people there. Only the sounds of nature could be heard and it reminded me of what Billy said about moments after the shooting. We knew when the coffin was coming down by the commands of the sergeant to the Guard of Honour, making them stand to attention. It was only then that the silence was broken. We could hear the sounds of people starting to cry as Daddy's coffin draped in the union flag appeared from the front door. The six coffin bearers made their way towards us with the Reverend Brown leading them in verse from the Bible. At this stage, Mummy was in bits and had to be helped by her sisters. They held her with both arms and were crying at the same time. Aunty Mary took Boyd from her arms, because she most likely would have dropped him.

They reached the hearse and we thought they would put Daddy inside. No, with the church only a mile or so away they decided to carry Daddy the whole way with different groups of men taking a lift. The UDR men carried the coffin behind the hearse down the drive before coming to a stop and changing lifters. As they were changing, I could hear Root in the background barking away as if he knew what was going on and just imagined Daddy saying, "Root, go to bed," as he always had to. This time, it was Daddy's brothers who would take the lift. Uncles Sam, Jimmy, George, Alan, Trevor and

Daddy's best friend Roy. They carried the coffin out of sight of the house before some of Mummy's family took a lift. Uncles John, Sean, Roy, Pat, Jack and Paddy. There were two more lifts mostly of Daddy's friends, some of which I didn't know. Then as we got to the church gates the UDR men took the last lift to take Daddy into the church. As we got closer, we could hear one bell toll every ten or so seconds. It became louder and louder the closer we got. The rooks and crows in the trees began to fill the sky with sound and that peaceful feeling that our church has disappeared for the moment to the sound of thousands of people walking up the drive to the church. When we got to the church door, we paused for a moment. The Reverend Brown then led the coffin in again, as he did at our home, with scriptures from the bible. The church was full already, except for the seats reserved for family. Mummy was in a bad, bad way as we were led to our seats. I looked at the floor for a good few moments because I was trying to be brave for Mummy. I lifted my head to Daddy's coffin in place at the front. The only thing I remember from that service was looking around at the memorial plaques on the walls to fallen soldiers of WW1 and WW2. The one other thing was a verse from one of Daddy's favourite poems. He often would recite poetry to us. Aunty Margaret read it out because of her background in her local church.

W.F. Marshall's *Tullyneil.*

> On that green hill in dark Tyrone
>
> That lifts its shoulders broad
>
> Above a house of weathered stone
>
> -A plain old house of God-
>
> The whins embroider now the lea,
>
> The cattle come and go,
>
> Crab-apple blossom, fair to see

Warms up the whitethorn snow.

Speaker after speaker praised Daddy for the man he was, but it was all a blur after Aunty Margaret. Before I knew it, we were singing the last hymn, 'Abide With Me'. Daddy was aloft again and making his way out of the church. We all fell into place behind the coffin. I was holding onto John and James to Billy. Mum had Boyd back in her arms. Mummy whispered to us as we got up, "Heads high, boys, for your daddy." That's just what we did. We all felt as if Daddy was expecting us to be proud young men and do Mummy proud in front of so many people.

'Abide With Me' was still filling the church with voices that made us feel strong. The choir, which was all local people and family friends, sung through the tears. As we reached the edge of the doorway, the coffin stopped for a moment. I looked up and the sun blinded us, reflecting off Daddy's name plate on his coffin. It made me feel like Daddy shone a light on us to tell us he was looking over us today. Then the reason we stopped was made clear. A single piper filled his lungs and led Daddy to his resting place. We walked out into a beautiful winter's sunshine. A sharp breeze on the trees, although bare of leaves, was still making an eerie sound with the rooks in full voice. We got to the edge of the gravel path and watched the UDR men make their way on the grass to the plot. They stopped on each side of the plot before turning in and facing each other. They lowered together, and as soon as they stood up, the piper ended. For a moment, that eerie sound took over and it seemed like the Reverend let it. From this point, what was said was a total blur. All we could do was just stare at Daddy's coffin knowing that this would be the last time we would be next to him in body. My recollection began again when Mummy leaned over and put a rose on top of the coffin before the soldiers started to lower him down. That's when it really hit us that this was goodbye. We all grabbed each other as the coffin lowered and cried our hearts out. Aunty Mary was holding Mum who was still holding Boyd in her arms. Mummy began to cry Daddy's name and it carried through the air. When it was lowered, the soldiers removed their lowering ropes and marched away. The five of us boys then dropped a rose in and said our final goodbye. Within moments, a volley of shots cut through the air and frightened us to death. Billy, in particular, did not like this as he suffered the same feeling when Daddy's car was attacked. There was a volley of three shots before we could hear the sergeant called his command. The next twenty minutes we spent shaking hands of well-wishers round the grave. Again, it's just a blur seeing face after face passing on their sorrow. After they had stopped, we spent a few minutes as a family over the grave. We just looked at the mountain of flowers piled on top of the grave and just knew that Daddy was well loved.

Before we turned and left, Mummy said to us, "I'm proud of you all boys. You did your daddy proud. He will be looking down with a smile of joy and pride at how you all were today and remember, you all have your father's blood running through your veins. But I want every one of you to promise me one thing before we leave Daddy." She knelt down beside us and looked at every one of us in turn. "I want you to promise me that, until your dying day, you will seek to find out who took your daddy from us. You will seek them out and have our revenge. I don't care how long it takes but the killers will pay for what they have done to us all. Promise me." In turn, every one of us made that promise to Mummy. She kissed us, stood up and said quietly, "Someday, William, I will be with you again but until that day, my love, please guide us on the right path. Sweet dreams, my darling William." We turned and walked away hand in hand knowing that a new journey in life was now laid out for us.

As we got to the hall which was full of family, friends and well-wishers, politicians, UDR and RUC, they all wanted to wish us well and pay their respects. There was an endless stream of people waiting in turn. Mummy could see that we were getting tired and a bit overwhelmed with the whole day and decided that she would take us home and then on to the County Hospital to see Sammy, after we had something to eat and drink which took about thirty minutes. James then came over and said Mummy wants us all at the front. The five of us and Mummy stood there waiting for everyone to hush before Mummy spoke to all there. "I want to thank you all for your love and support of the last three days. Without you all, we would have never made it through these awful days. I look at our families here and I can't thank you enough for what you did to help. The boys thank you as well but we have a little boy in hospital fighting for his life that we want to be with now. I would like you all if you could to pray for Sammy and to help him make it through. He will need all of God's help. Thank you all from the bottom of our hearts, thank you."

As we started to leave, not one voice spoke. All that was heard was crying. We walked through the mass of people looking at us in pure sadness. The vision of a mother walking hand in hand with five young children through that hall would have made the hardest of hard men weep. We made our way down the front stairs where Uncle Jimmy and Uncle Sam were waiting to take us to the County Hospital to see Sammy. When the doors to the car closed, we all started crying and never spoke. The pressure of it all had finally gotten to us.

As we got out of the car at the hospital, we were greeted by the nurses looking after Sammy. She spoke to Mummy and told her that Sammy had come out of his coma around 1.30 p.m. That was the same time that Daddy was buried. Why? Who knows if there is a reason to this? We didn't care at the moment. We made our way in to him where we were all greeted with a smile on his face. Sammy was going to be okay. Daddy took care of that. The next hard step was telling Sammy Daddy was gone.

Chapter 6
Life Without My One True Love

Life without Daddy was not going to be easy for us boys but for Mummy it was devastating. He was her rock in many ways. He was a man who would stand up for what's right as a husband and father. On many occasions he stepped up to make sure Mummy didn't get any shit because she married a Protestant. A lot of the shit Mummy never got to know about. On quite a few occasions Daddy was approached by people sent by Granny D to talk him out of marrying Mummy and on every occasion that person got what was coming, man or woman. Daddy was arrested once for beating up two men in a pub after an altercation about Mummy being a Catholic. The two men decided that Daddy was a disgrace to his religion and community for marrying a taig. Taig is another slang word for Catholic. They were both local loyalists who thought they were the hard men from the Cross area. Daddy did eventually catch up with them and the only thing hard about those two was how hard they hit the ground, and didn't get back up in a hurry either. He waited until they thought they got away with it and he showed them what a hard man looks and feels like. Not one person in the pub that night would step up to help them out but what they did do was to do nothing. The police arrived and took two statements. The only two statements they got were from the two not-so-hard men. Now that wasn't why Daddy was arrested. The not so hard men ended up in an alleyway knee capped a few days later. We don't know who did the knee capping but the man who spoke to us at Daddy's funeral about helping us out whenever it was needed was suspect number one. Daddy was asked his whereabouts that night and he had a strong alibi. He was on duty with the UDR. The not-so-hard men weren't seen in the Cross again. Mummy was never told of this until Daddy was dead. The same thing happened with a couple of Republicans trying it on with Daddy and his friends one night at a pub snooker match. They didn't walk away either. From what we have been told about this incident, the two Republicans asked Daddy why he didn't marry one of his own kind and leave their girls alone. That comment was met with fury and anger. Daddy had a group of friends that were pure old school hard men. They used fists and feet and not knives or guns. They left a lot of damaged men in their wake that never really recovered from the beating they took. Did that image and reputation add to Daddy being targeted? Who knows, but, needless to say, he and his group of mates were well known in the Tyrone area. I think Mummy relied on Daddy having her back for a lot of things. He was the money earner and ran the successful farm that they had. He not only had the farm but ran the tractor and farmyard machinery business as well.

Although life after Daddy for Mummy was never going to be easy, she always did her best to protect us boys from harm and gossip. She would always talk and comfort us when we felt down and if nasty people said nasty things. We got some abuse from kids at school about the fact that Mummy was a Catholic—a fact that was only known because of the press and TV putting it out that Daddy was in a mixed marriage. They just didn't know the trouble they caused by reporting such news. Mummy spent a lot of time being called to the school to explain why her sons were always fighting other kids at school. Most of the trouble was some children thought it was okay to tease us about Mummy being a Catholic and on every occasion the children involved got a good slap. She never, ever stepped back and said sorry for what we did. She always backed us up saying, "My boys wouldn't be fighting if you did your job, teacher. Why aren't you sorting out the big mouths who keep saying things to my boys and making them fight?" On each occasion, she left that school with a promise that the school would do their best to stop the nasty rumours and nasty comments. That never worked; it just kept happening to us. James spent a lot of time being expelled from school for fighting and standing his ground which meant Mummy spent a lot of time in the school defending him. She was like a bull in a china shop when she was in the head's office. It took a couple of years before it stopped but by that time we all had a bad reputation at school and even the younger of us had a bad reputation even before they got to the big school. The one of us that never stepped back in any way at all was Billy. He had yet at this stage to go to the big school but when he did get to the big school they knew about it. He had a serious issue with anyone who tried to bring up what we had gone through. I think the reason why it got better at school for us is that Billy started. One thing for sure is that we had each other's backs.

Mummy tried her best to stop us from fighting, but she knew the reason we did and had an understanding of why we did it. Mummy never had another relationship which I think made her very lonely. We often asked her if she ever wanted to meet another man and she always was prompt in saying no, not at all. We believed her. The home farm suffered in the first year after Daddy's death, but with our uncles doing their best to help out, it survived. Daddy's tractor shop business was handed to Uncle Alan to look after until Sammy and James were old enough to take over. They did spend most weekends helping out and learning the business. Mummy did visit the shop often, but she was more like a silent owner. As the first year ended, Mummy decided that time had come to get her life on track. She started to spend most of her free time working on the farm but she needed help from Uncle Sam who took over Grandad R's farm. He would call at the farm and carry out most of the heavy work. He also took on some of the empty fields and put his livestock to graze on them. Mummy and Uncle Sam had an agreement about his help on the farm. This was that he could use our fields free. That worked out well for both of them. When all the boys were at school she had the free time to work on the farm. She started to take on more sheep and chickens on the farm which was easier for her to handle alone, and whenever we finished school, we all had our jobs to do. We would never let Mummy down and shirk our responsibilities on the farm, plus we all enjoyed the farming life. With the passing of a year, we all began to cope better at home but that time of the year that we would never forget was coming around for the first time. One of the family circle that we overlooked in that first year was Daddy's dog, Root. We were so wound up in our own thoughts that we all thought someone else was looking after Root. He was always fed and watered but just never got any attention. On a few occasions, he got loose, and we would always find him sitting on Daddy's grave. I took him there on the lead a few times to see Daddy's resting place, so I suppose he knew where he was buried. Root was in mourning just like the rest of us and missed his master. December the 10th—the day Daddy was killed. Mummy always got very quiet on the run up to that date and would sometimes show some anger towards us, but we never let it get to us as we were the same with each other. The first year, we had a lot of family visiting us from both Mummy and Daddy's families but the elephant in the room was always the same. No Granny D. Mind you, I don't think Mummy wanted her to visit us anyway. Mummy's family were split on her actions with some of her brothers and sisters still not talking to Granny D.

We didn't really think about Christmas in the first years after Daddy's death as there was nothing to celebrate in our eyes. We did put a Christmas tree up, but it just didn't look festive. Truthfully, it looked like shit. Daddy's first anniversary was on a Wednesday, so we decided to have a church service on the Sunday before. It was also the same time as the military grave headstone was put on Daddy's grave. Before Daddy's death, I remember seeing other military headstones in graveyard wondering what they were. I learnt that lesson very quickly. The church that day in the Cross was full to capacity on the Sunday morning with all of the same faces that were at the funeral service. There were both Catholic and Protestants in attendance that day, which was great to see. Even though it was one year on, it was still very raw in our minds. Boyd and John started to show some feelings about Daddy but still did not have strong memories of him. The rest of us still had a hard time dealing with the memories flooding back.

Some of Mummy's family were there and showed us a lot of support. Uncle Paddy was his usual self with us, very funny and trying to make us smile a bit and as usual giving us sweets. Some of Mummy's brothers and sisters didn't show up. It was not a surprise when you look back now but then it was noticed that they did not turn up. We did know that some of them did take Granny D's side in the row. They turned out to be supporters of the Republican struggle. It was very obvious to us that they did. We once noticed on TV one of them at the funeral of two IRA men that were killed by their own bomb. We always thought the reason we didn't see more of them was because the rest of them were in IRA uniform and wearing a balaclava. There were a lot of IRA deaths in the Tyrone area, be it at their own hands or the security forces, so the likelihood of that being the case was strong. Own goals as we called it did happen often, and when they did, nearly all of the Protestant community and some of the Catholic community celebrated. In the nearby village, one Catholic lad was kneecapped because he openly laughed about such an event. It was not talked about in such away in public again by that community. At the service, the local priest was there and showed community togetherness by getting up and saying the Lord's Prayer with us. Some in the church didn't like that, because a week or so before Daddy's anniversary, he gave service to an IRA man killed by a police officer as he and two others tried to kill the off-duty policeman. The officer in question was able to fire back and showed his training worked well. He killed one and wounded one other. He was not hit, and this incident just goes to show the IRA can't handle it when their target shoots back. Nevertheless, it was a gesture that was welcomed by the family as a whole. As the service came to an end, we all listened to the local piper as he played Amazing Grace. He was standing at the top of the church which made the pipes echo throughout the church. Mummy led us out, as she did a year before, to Daddy's graveside but this time a headstone bore the name of Daddy. We stood at the grave as a family, knowing that there where hundreds of people watching us. The sadness in the church graveyard was so obvious, even though it was a year on. Mummy laid a bunch of red roses beside the headstone and we all followed by laying one single white rose along the grave. Six white roses and twelve red roses. We did the same thing every year and on his anniversary. A member of the UDR approached us with a UDR wreath and asked permission to lay the wreath. It was one of Daddy's platoon leaders and the same man who took control of the UDR men at Daddy's funeral. He whispered to us that our dad would never be forgotten in the ranks of the UDR. That made all of us boys feel very proud. As the people dispersed from the graveyard, we all stayed at the graveside looking at the same wreaths we did a year before. They were well weathered, but we just didn't want to just remove them and put them in the bin. We all put our hands on the new gravestone as Mummy asked us to. For a moment we stood silent and then Mummy spoke. "We still miss you, darling, every day and pray that you are looking down on us with pride. Help us in our hour of need and come to us in our dreams, darling William." Boyd and John looked up at Mummy, wondering what she meant by that but never asked her. We tried to explain to them later, but they were just too young to understand. When we decided to leave the graveyard, we found that nearly everyone had left. We didn't realise how long we stood at the grave. We walked home hand in hand as we did a year ago but this time we talked to each other. Mummy was very talkative to us this time telling us how it was time to get this family life back on track. "Now listen boys, it's about time you all started to be good at school and don't let them big mouth frigers get to you. I'm not having people talk about us anymore. We'll show them, do you hear me now. It's time to show your daddy we are going to be okay. I'm relaying on you bigger cubs to help the weans through this." We all just listened and never spoke. Many nights we listened to Mummy cry on her own and it was so upsetting to us all. We would all end up in the hallway outside her door just sitting, listening and crying for her. Sometimes we would go into her room as she sounded so very upset. If and when we did, we just got on her bed and hugged her. Sometimes, we ended up listening to funny stories some of us would tell. We did laugh sometimes, which lifted Mummy's spirits. On many a morning, we all woke up in her bed and Mummy would be downstairs starting her usual chores. She would get up, leave us sleeping and just carry on. That was Mummy's way. As soon as she heard us move in her bedroom, she would be shouting for us to get up and if it was the weekend it would be an early shout. "Come on you lot, time to get up. Jobs to be done," she would shout, and if it was a school day she would shout, "Get up now you lot, if you miss that bloody bus you'll be walking to school." We often heard Uncle Sam start work in the yard before we even thought about getting up, but when we heard the sound of the Grey Fergie starting up, it was up and at it for us. We all loved working on the farm, each and every one of us. Summer time was so much fun on the farm. Lots to do all day long and we did it with a smile on our faces. Me? Even when I went off to stay with Aunty Sally's family for two or three weeks in the summer, it was to another farm. It did look at one time every one of us would became farmers when we became men. As the first year ended and the second year without Daddy began, we started to cope with what life had to offer us a little bit easier. Don't get me wrong; it was still hard for us to cope in the outside world with all the killing but we all found it easier within the family circle. I suppose that's why we spent a lot of our time on the farm playing and working. We got on really well with one another, with little or no arguments. Mummy was never hard on us, but if she needed to be she would. It was always the same issues and problems that she would have to sort out. It was always the problems we had at school. We didn't have the same problems in the Cross even when we played in the parks or played football or rugby with the local children. It was only at school. Mummy would always say,

"Children can be nasty without even thinking about it. That's why you can never do or say as they do or say."

We could walk around the Cross knowing we wouldn't have any problems and Mummy would never shy away from living a normal life. It was as if she got Daddy's inner strength to carry on. It wasn't the same when we went to other towns or villages though. Mummy always felt like people talked about her when she showed her face in town. They were, but mostly in sorrow for a mother of six boys who lost her husband to the troubles, but Mummy would never show it. On one occasion, Mummy met the local priest while visiting the post office and he stopped to talk to her for a while. As he did, Granny D just happened to be on the same street going to the same post office. She walked in, saw them talking and just turned around and walked out again. Not one word was spoken to Mummy or the priest. That didn't go down well with the priest, as Granny D was never out of the chapel praying and getting involved in everything that went on in the village. Apparently, the look on his face was enough to scare the shit out of a nun. The priest told Mummy he was sorry for the dilemma she was in and that he would do his best to make Granny D change her views and ways. Mummy was so hardened to it now that meetings like this become like water off a duck's back. She always told us that we were better off not having Granny D and her cronies in our lives. We always agreed. Out of Mummy's brothers and sisters there were only three we knew Mummy could talk to and trust: Joyce, Mary and Sean. The rest Mummy didn't trust in any way. She could, however, trust Grandad D. He took it hard when Daddy was killed as he had a close friend in Daddy because they had a common interest and hobby—old grey Fergie tractors. They would spend many an evening out in the sheds working on their Massey's and talking the night away. Sometimes, there would be up to ten men out there talking nothing but tractors. Mummy would be busy carrying tea and sandwiches out to them all evening long. She did join in sometimes because the craic was good. Not long after Daddy was taken from us, he offered to buy our grey Fergie because of the amount of work he and Daddy put into it. Thankfully, Mummy said no to him. He was okay with Mummy's answer and offered to buy it if we ever decided to sell it. We needed it to work on the farm and the old girl never gives us any trouble.

Grandad D didn't come around as much now, which upset Mummy a little. She enjoyed his company and I suppose the fact that he introduced Daddy to Mummy which led to the marriage meant that he approved and was okay with his Catholic daughter marrying a Protestant man. It felt like when he did visit it was only to use Daddy's work shop which had all the tools he needed to repair his tractor.

Mummy didn't mind, though, as long as she got to see him. They never talked about Granny D because it would end in an argument that no one would or could win but still, they had a good father-daughter relationship. One thing that upset Mummy was when it was her parent's 50th wedding anniversary and Mummy wasn't invited. They had a big party in the local church hall with all of the family circle invited. That was except us. Some of Mummy's friends left when they found out that we were not invited, and the priest did kind of point that out when he was asked to say prayers. He asked everyone to pray for the victims of the ongoing troubles and for the whole Darcy family in attendance and those that were not. He had a sharp look at Granny D at the moment he said, "Those that were not." Everyone there knew exactly what he meant, and it left the party-goers with a bitter resentment towards either him or Granny D. I suppose it depended on whether you supported the IRA struggle or you had a hatred for the men of violence destroying the country. It seemed to leave the celebrations a bit dull and half the invites left half way through the night. It was the talk of the town for a week or so after which made Mummy feel embarrassed but just like the woman she was she dusted herself down, so to speak, and got on with looking after her own family. That was her only focus in life now. Through all the troubles that were going on around us, we never let it slip what we as a family had to do. We all focused on the road ahead and on each other, plus we always tried to do what was best for us all and to do what Daddy would have wanted us to do.

Mummy always said to us, "Never forget, boys; your daddy is only a dream away and will always be looking down on you to make sure you're on the right track in life. He will always be our guardian angel up in heaven." That was something we believed in and would never forget. In times of need, we relied on our guardian angel. Even today, I have the same feeling, but now I feel I have two guardian angels to guide me through. It's a comfort knowing I'm never alone in good and bad times. As the years rolled on and some of us became young men, you would think that our priorities would change. That just never happened. We surrounded Mummy with love and comfort and never let her down. She would always refer to us as my boys and no matter what we did she would support us and defend us against anyone. Of course, when we were at home she was different, we got a good telling off if what we did was bad. That was her way and a way that made us love her even more. As James and Sammy became men, no one ever bad mouthed her again. They both become hard and honest men just like Daddy was. His reputation was now theirs and people knew it. Mummy was again back in the safe place knowing that Richards's men had her back. Ten years on from Daddy's death, we would still on some occasions find Mummy crying at night and we would still find ourselves in the hallway listening to her. We just showed her all the love we could. Another very sad time was about to be upon us when Daddy's dog Root got to the end of his life with us. Root was brought into the family as an 8-week-old puppy and was to become the best dog Daddy ever had, and, between the families, we had a lot of dogs. Root was a well-trained gun dog only used when the men went out on shoots. As children we were not to go near him while he was being trained so that Root was a one-man dog. We all knew it was coming, but when it did, it was heart breaking. Boyd found him under Daddy's grey Fergie looking like he was fast asleep but he wasn't. He crawled under the tractor as he did many times with Daddy and just went to sleep where he always did when Daddy was working on the tractor. Boyd first called us all over to see Root before he moved him because it looked like he was so peaceful at his ending. We took Root out to the back of the barn and buried him where he used to stand and watch the sheep. It felt like another part of Daddy was gone. One thing I did notice at that time was Sammy became very distant and spent more and more time on his own. I told Mummy about my thoughts and she agreed but said just give him space and that we all had our moments where we needed our own space at times. Looking back, I wish I had talked to him more. At the end of the eighties and the troubles still in full flow some of us boys became men and left our teenage years behind us. We all changed in different ways but still had one thing in common. Mummy was that common cause. She had six lads that had her back, no matter what. As we grew older, our determination and commitment grew with it. We hadn't forgotten our pledge at Daddy's graveside and the promise we all made to Mummy.

Chapter 7
Six Boys Become Six Men

1980 had started with yet more deaths in Ulster. More British and UDR soldiers, more RUC men killed and even more innocent people who were caught up in somebody else's war murdered without a care. The numbers of Terrorists deaths grew as well which didn't sadden us at all. Terrorists from both communities were hiding in plain sight. The RUC knew who was doing what but not necessarily when. It was common knowledge that the British SAS were working in most areas of Ulster taking on the IRA at their own game. Hide behind a hedge and ambush them. There was no doubt that they had a 'shoot to kill and answer questions later' policy. For our community, we agreed to this policy as it was our community that the IRA were murdering on a daily basis. As with most families in Ulster, affected or not with life here, we all on both sides learned to live with the troubles. Just another day was how most lived. I remember Uncle Alan saying something to me that was, no more than a throw away comment of what a terrorist would think and say. It was a comment that stuck in my mind for a long time. "Bury your dead 'cause there's plenty more where they come from." The sentiment was very true. As the years came and went, we all changed in many ways. There was ten years between the six of us and if you count Richie our brother who died at birth it was ten years between seven of us. In 1979, when Daddy was killed, James was thirteen years old, Sammy twelve, Stephen (me) ten, Billy nine, Richie would have been seven, John five and Boyd three. Both John and Boyd have little memories of Daddy but as they both say, "At least we can remember his face and

83

smile." That was something we all had. When Daddy died, both James and Sammy were at an age where they started to work with Daddy, whether it be on the farm or at the tractor shop. When I say work, it was more like just hanging out with Daddy. He would give us jobs to do around the farm or shop which we all loved doing. I suppose that's why we all wanted to go with Daddy at the weekends. Their memories of Daddy were stronger than the rest of us. I do have lots of memories which I try to hang onto, but as time fades, so do the memories. Billy, on the other hand, is a bit in between. More than Boyd and John but less than James, Sammy and me. We all thought that we would never lose our memories of Daddy but, as I said, with time, we did. It took a lot of time for both Sammy and Billy to recover from the shooting but more so Sammy. Sammy was shot three times and would have bad memories about that day for years to come. He also spent his life in constant pain from the gunshot wound to his leg. Not much helped him with his pain. The one thing that did help him with the pain would end up only helping to kill him, but we didn't know that until it was too late. The journey we all took into manhood always had Mummy at the heart of everything—what she needed, what she wanted and what she had. No one, be it a lover or wife, would come between us and Mummy. As individuals we all grew up the same, but when you look into each one of us, we were as different as chalk and cheese.

First Born

James

Being the first born in any family, you become the special one in many ways not only to your parents but to the grandparents as well. James was the first boy born in the Richards family and not only that, Daddy was also the first son in his family to have a boy. Needless to say, he was a bit spoilt by Granny and Grandad R. He spent a lot of time out at the family home with Grandad on the farm. Uncle Billy and James spent a lot of time together on the farm and whenever James was on the farm you would most likely find him working with Uncle Alan. The rest of us got to spend time on the farm as well but not as much as James. Whenever Mummy and Daddy needed a babysitter, they only had to ask him. It never seemed to be a problem. When Daddy joined the UDR, James was always first to help him with his uniform. He would become one hell of a boot polisher. I remember Daddy always saying, "Who's going to spit and polish my boots, cubs?" James was always first to say, "I will, Daddy." Sammy and I would only get the chance if James was somewhere else, usually at Grandad's farm. When it came to cleaning his gun, which was usually an SLR (Self-Loading Rifle), Daddy would only let us watch, that was until we were big enough to understand its dangers. I remember James getting the chance to clean it for the first time. He was like a duck taking to water. Daddy would always make us watch as he unloaded the gun again and again to show it was safe and ready to be stripped and cleaned. In one instance, James did something that could have killed someone and something that would make Daddy and Mummy be more than careful about the guns in the house. Daddy came home from patrol one Sunday morning after being out overnight. He had left his gun in the scullery with his Burgan and most of his UDR uniform. He was in a hurry because he was meeting up with Grandad D to go to a tractor show in Belfast. He was running late. I remember James shouting, "I'll clean your boots, Daddy," and Daddy shouting back as he left the house, "Good lad. They're in the scullery." We didn't think anything of it as we did it so often. Even Mummy never flinched. As soon as Daddy left, James rushed into the scullery to clean his boots. We were in the living room and Mummy was outside gathering eggs and none of us knew what James was really up to. When he had finished cleaning the boots, he picked up Daddy's SLR and began to pretend he was Daddy. To be honest, we all have picked up a stick and pretended to be Daddy with his gun. It's what children do. He took the gun out the back door and pretended to shoot the chickens. Mummy was just around the corner, so she never saw him. James didn't know it but Daddy didn't empty the chamber because of the rush he was in. BANG. The next noise was the chickens running like hell and Mummy turning the corner. The eggs didn't make it this time. She looked at James with shock, not knowing what just happened. He dropped the gun and looked at Mummy as if to say it wasn't me. She ran over, grabbed him by the arm and dragged him into the scullery. He got a couple of hard slaps to the back of the head and was told to sit down at the table. She went out, picked up the SLR and checked the gun for another round. She knew how to handle the gun safely. Luckily for James, there was only one round in the gun as Daddy had already took the mag out. UDR men never unloaded their gun until they were inside their houses just in case of an attack on them. They had to be ready at all times. Sammy, Billy and myself were in the scullery wondering what was going on when Mummy walked past us, SLR in hand, and not a word out of her. James was in the kitchen sitting alone with a grey face knowing he was in a world of trouble. Mummy shouted to us to go outside and play, and we knew that when she shouted like that we got up and went outside immediately. I looked back, and James was staring at the floor waiting for what was to come. We could hear the shouting outside the house but didn't want to get beat so we went out to the field to kick a ball around. Five minutes later, Mummy came out and went back to collecting eggs. She was muttering away to the chickens, or to herself, obviously very angry with James. "Sammy, SAMMY, get inside and look after John and Boyd now." Sammy stopped, looked over at her. "Now, I said." He dropped the ball and ran inside. We followed a few minutes later and James was still sitting at the table with his homework book in front of him and crying.

"What did you do?" I asked. He fired his pencil at me and told me to go away, so I ran into the front room where Sammy was.

"What did he do?" Sammy asked.

"I don't know but he threw a pencil at me." We only found out later when Daddy come home what he did.

As soon as he got in the door, Mummy started on him. "What the fuck were you thinking, leaving your gun loaded where the cubs could get to it, William? James took it outside and fired a bloody shot at the chickens. He could have killed someone, you stupid bastard."

"You're fucking joking me," Daddy said. "The wee shit. Where is he?"

"He's upstairs in the back room." Daddy stormed upstairs, grabbed James and took him outside to the barn. The noise of them coming down the stairs was so loud. We didn't hear what he said or did to him, but we knew that it wasn't going to be good. He got beaten with the dreaded leather belt and grounded for two weeks. He didn't get to clean Daddy's boots for a while after that. Sammy was the one who got to clean the boots. About three weeks later, Daddy took James, Sammy and myself to the shooting range to show us what a loaded gun could do. Our thoughts of guns before we witnessed the ferociousness of what a gun could really do was just great, and we couldn't wait to shoot one for real. "Right boys. Lie down on that bank behind me and watch. Do you see that square shape target to the left of that old car down at the tree line? Watch it closely." Unbeknown to us, Uncle Jimmy was behind us with his SLR loaded and ready. Before Daddy got to finish the word 'closely', Uncle Jimmy let loose with rapid fire. It seemed to go on for ever but was only about ten seconds long. We never saw the target because our noses were stuck in the dirt with our hands covering our ears. When it stopped, we looked back to see Uncle Jimmy laughing and reloading at the same time. Seconds later, Daddy, who was standing in front of us, opened up on the same target. This time we did see a bit of it but only because he had shorter bursts. The old car was completely destroyed and the target to the left of the car was untouched. I started to cry with fear at one stage but soon stopped when James told me to shut up. For us all, the first burst of fire scared the shit out of us. I can't emphasise enough how much it scared us. Even James after his mishap and who had seen more of guns than Sammy and I was affected by it. Some might say Daddy was careless in the way he did it, but it had the right effect on us.

"What do you think of that?" Uncle Jimmy asked. Sammy and I were dumfounded at the noise, let alone the damage to the car. James, on the other hand, was laughing and asking them to do it again.

"Now that's what a gun can do to a car from this range, cubs. Imagine what it could do to a car with a person in it up close. I want you to remember what a gun can do in the hands of anyone, let alone a madman's hands." He handed his gun to Uncle Jimmy and knelt down beside us and with an angry-looking face he said sharply, "THIS IS NOT A TOY. DON'T EVER FORGET THAT." James's laughing stopped as he knew it was directed at him. "Right, James, over here now. I want you to lie down here." Uncle Jimmy handed Daddy a 2.2 rifle and started to show him how to use a gun. We watched and waited eagerly to have a turn. "You have five rounds to hit the target to the left of the car. Relax and try to keep the gun steady." The look on James's face was of pure excitement and all that happened in the last few weeks was forgotten for the moment. He hit the target twice out of five shots which was good for his first time. As he got up, he had a great big smile on his face but it kind of changed when Uncle Jimmy said, "Do you think you could do better if there was chickens down there, Jimmy boy?" We all laughed a bit, but James didn't. "Sammy, you're next. Same thing, five shots on the target." Again, like James, Sammy had a big grin on his face. He hit the target only once, but he didn't mind. "Right come on Stephen, you're next. Five shots." I missed with all five shots, but it was so much fun I didn't care.

On the way home, Uncle Jimmy give us a pep talk on guns in general and we listened to every word he said. "So, James, do you think you will pick up your Daddy's gun again and shoot at the chickens?"

"No way," he shouted back.

"Good lad but see if you do, you will go to jail and be known as the chicken killer. That wouldn't be good, would it?" He shook his head no. Sammy and I laughed, but James didn't see the funny side of it. Sammy got a dig in the ribs from him. When we got home he went straight into the kitchen where Mummy was and was asked by her how it went today. We learned an important lesson that day and never forgot it.

Through all the trouble James got into at school for fighting, he never became a bad lad. He stood his ground when people had a dig about Mummy being a Catholic. He didn't have a father figure to show him his wrong ways but then neither did the rest of us so we all travelled the same road. He did well at school and went on to the Tec where he studied engineering. He spent a lot of time at the tractor garage with Daddy before he died and then carried on working there with Uncle Alan. He eventually took over the machinery side of the business, but Uncle Alan was still the man in charge of the financial side and it stayed that way for a long time. James did become more experienced in that side of the business but as Mummy said why change a good thing. She was a silent owner and would hand over the reins when James and Sammy were at the right age and had the right experience to run the place. On his 25th birthday, James got married to a great girl call Jane. She was from Omagh, and he met her at Tec but didn't ask her out until they accidentally met at a wedding three years later. Four years later, they tied the knot. Mummy was so proud of him that day. She loved Jane and she became the daughter she never had. Mummy changed then because she knew the chances of having a grandchild were just around the corner. The day they told Mummy Jane was with child was by far the happiest day to date, and if that wasn't enough, Jane gave birth to a baby girl. James was over the moon and the one thing that he wanted to do was to name the new born after Daddy or Mummy. This time it was Mummy. Rose-Ann Richards—the first grandchild and Daddy would have been so proud of them. The day after Rose-Ann was born, she got out of hospital and the whole family visited Daddy's grave with her. Mummy introduced her to Daddy as if he was standing beside her. It was so touching and sad to see her standing there feeling so proud of James. Jane and her whole family who were with us were so touched. That day they understood how close of a family we were. They built a house on the farm land next to Mummy's house and the area become the family home to quite a few houses. They had another two children in the next three years. A boy William Billy, named after Daddy, and a girl Sarah-Jane, named after Jane's mum. Mummy was in her element with a new lease on life with three grandchildren so close to home and not once did they ever have a bad word for each other. She loved Jane like a daughter. It's not often you get two families who get on together so well. Jane's family was great. Every one of them. What's that old saying, it's a marriage made in heaven. James and Jane had that. With the shop doing well for him and his family complete, James become the man Daddy was turning into. The day that Rose-Ann was born Mummy said to him, "I always knew you were your daddy's son. You have his strength and willpower that he worked so hard to instil in you all from the day you were born." Life was good for James and his new family.

Second Born

Sammy

After all his troubles in life, Sammy always did the best with what he had been handed in life. Shot three times at the age of twelve and in constant pain from his leg wound, he never moaned, complained or used his situation to gain anything. He just ploughed on and lived his life the best way he could, but it was hard on him. He was the second born to Mummy and Daddy and had issues at birth. It wasn't as bad as it could have been. Luckily enough, the doctor had seen the signs when Mummy was in labour and acted quick enough to ensure he made it. He spent six days in the hospital, gaining strength every day, and after a few months, he was as normal as any baby at two months old. He was named after Mummy's daddy, which made Grandad D very proud. I can't say the same of Granny D though. She hated it and would never utter his name. We know that because Mummy's sisters often talked about it when they visited. Because of Sammy having issues with his birth, he become the apple of Daddy's eye and not only that, Aunty Mary made him her little miracle prince. She would always show him a lot of love and attention and took him whenever Mummy needed some help. She was so good to us all and we looked forward to her visits. Even when she had her own family of two girls, she always looked after Sammy when she needed to. Sammy was twelve when Daddy died and was in the car when it happened. He was three times, twice in the leg and once in the belly. The leg injury never got much better and gave him pain for the rest of his life. He didn't get to say goodbye to Daddy as he was so poorly, in hospital. His last image of Daddy was him singing along to George Harrison's song, My Sweet Lord, on the radio. He looked at him in the rear mirror making sure he was singing along. He would always refer to it as the do-do song because of Daddy wanting him and Billy to sing along. Even though the song had bad memories tied to it for him, he loved the song and always sang along to it when he heard it. It was their song, Daddy, Sammy and Billy's. He did very well at school and followed in James's footsteps, passing their eleven plus exams which pleased Mummy and Daddy.

Grandad D would take him out on his grey Fergie and let him steer the tractor when he was in the fields. Mummy would often tell funny stories of Sammy driving around the fields on Grandad D's tractor turning the steering from left to right as fast as possible but going in a straight line; not only that, it was the way he laughed when he had seen us watching and laughing at him. She said he would cackle like a goat, and if you went near him to help out, he would growl at you to get off. She would act out the part like he did, and it was so funny. Many a night we heard this story and it was funny every time. That was the fun we had on the farm and why we loved it. Sammy always had a certain look about him—jet black hair which shined in the sunshine like a mirror. He was often referred to as the little prince because of his looks. Granny D use to say he was the double of Daddy when Daddy was aged 10. The girls always said he was going to break so many hearts when he got older because of his good looks. As he got older, he started to cope well with his pains and stopped using and relying on medication so much. I remember Mummy many times sitting on the sofa with Sammy lying across her lap having cream rubbed into his leg and hip. The pain he went through at times made us all feel it. He was only a teenage boy who had to cope with so many different medical problems but got on with life the best he could. At school, he got some stick for having a bit of a limp and some were still having a go at him about Mummy's religion. He, like James, wasn't found wanting when those children came slagging them. Even with his injuries, he could hold his own, and if he couldn't, James had his back, and if it went further, Mummy was ready and willing to put the school and any student's parents in their place. Sammy was in his first six months at big school when Daddy died, which meant he missed about half of his first year either by not being able to make it to school or being in too much pain and had to go to the sick room to self-inject pain relief. James was often called to sit with him because he was so scared. He was sent home from school quite a lot in his first year. His concentration span was limited but he always tried his best. Aunty Mary spent so much time with him, trying to school him while he was at home. He never lost it with her as he did with school teachers and she never gave up on him, but saying that, the teachers were great as well. Some of them lost family members too. One of Sammy's teachers lost her father and husband in the same attack back in the seventies. She was someone we all turned to when we got into trouble. Sammy once told me about an incident after lunch time which the teacher got into trouble over. "I was on my way to class after lunch time one day when this year ten started to shout at me. He was mouthing off about Mummy being a taig and calling me a taig bastard. I didn't bite though 'cause I didn't want to have Mummy called in again. He started doing a stupid dance and he approached me singing the sash, asking me to join in yea wee taig fucker. What made him very angry was that I did join in and some in my class with me laughed at him. He stopped singing and came at me with a big haymaker. The fuckin post was quicker than him. It never reached me, because Mrs Trune intervened and kind of hit him on the nose with the handbag she was carrying. She led him away bloody nose and all to the head's office by the ear. I'm telling you it was by the bloody ear. It was bloody hilarious. She had to apologise to his family though.

"After that whenever we seen him, we would make it a point to shout 'Mrs Trune bloody nose him' at him. It was so funny and even funnier, a week later, James got him in the toilets and gave him a bloody nose again. Somehow I think that the stupid bastard learnt his lesson." That was Sammy all over. He could change a confrontation into a laugh, sometimes without even lifting his fists. Sammy had a heavy punch on him. I know, as he once punched me in the jaw. Jesus Christ, it hurt, and he was only 11 at the time. As James did, Sammy did well at big school and went on to the Tec. The difference about the Tec was that it had both Catholics and Protestants there. He never had any issues about who or what he was at the Tec, the same as James. I suppose the people who were at the Tec wanted to be there and only wanted to learn a trade. Sammy excelled there doing mechanical and engineering courses over three years. He, like James, was heading towards Daddy's business. By the time he had finished his City and Guilds, he had top marks and stepped into the business. He would learn the trade under Uncle Alan the same as James. Sammy would lean toward the repair side of the shop and James the sale, but they would both muck in wherever they had to. With the years of helping out when they were at school, they both hit the job running and fitted right in. As Sammy's first year at the shop ended, he began to show signs of frustration. He would spend his evenings out with one or two of his mates having a drink. It was not a problem as his work never faltered; he just seemed to be distant with us, well, except Mummy. She didn't see any problems with his ways. James, on the other hand, questioned his ways a few times but as I said his work never faltered. One night stood out when James called me and told me to meet him outside at the tractor barn. When I got there, he was waiting. "What's up, James?"

"It's Sammy," he said. "He's in trouble." I asked him what he meant. "He's been out drinking at some fucking disco and started fighting. Fucking McGoogans at the top of the town." Now this is a well-known Republican drinking hole and the last person you would think to find in it would be a Protestant.

"What the hell is he doing there?"

"I don't bloody know. Come on, we need to fetch him home before the police get him." By the time we got there, he had left, and no one would talk to us so we checked the first safe pub in the area and there he was. Not drunk or beat up much but a little banged up. James went straight up to him. "What's happened, Sammy, and what the fuck were you doing in McGoogan's bar? I just had a call from someone telling me you started a fight with two fellas in Celtic shirts."

He just looked at us and told us not to worry, that he didn't know where he was until it was too late. "Someone recognised me and tried to be a hero. Some fucking hero 'cause I knocked the cunt out with one punch. The other fucker did a runner when he saw his girlfriend having a nap." He started laughing as he told us the last bit and we just joined in laughing. He could be a funny fucker when he wanted, that boy. "Come on, lad, let's get you home." He was as good as gold. He got up and just left with us, thanking the bar staff as he did. When we got home he thanked us for the help and said goodnight. Mummy didn't know what happened which was a good thing because it's not something we would do to her. If we thought this was a one off, we were wrong, because two weeks later he was up to the same thing, only a different pub. On a Saturday morning, he came down the stairs stinking of booze and with a great big shiner. "That looks good, Sammy. What the hell have you been up to this time? I take it she said no a couple of times."

He grinned at us and said, "She did but I got my way after the third time of asking." Mummy laughed as if it was only a bit of fun, but I thought different. Later on, after he came home from the garage, I got the chance to ask him what was going on. Now he was okay with me, but I got the feeling he was hiding something from us.

"Seriously, Sammy, what's up lad? These last three weekends you've been out on the drink and coming home full out of your head and this story of a girl giving you a shiner is bollocks."

"Don't worry, Stephen. I'm just out having a bit of fun with the lads. I got a bit mouthy with a good-looking girl and her boyfriend slapped me from my bling spot. I didn't slap him back, because I was in the wrong."

"And what about all your drinking, Sammy? You're drinking a lot this last while and don't tell me it's only a bit of fun."

"I'm not drinking that much, Stephen; it's just that it doesn't take much to get me drunk these days." I had to believe him as he was very believable. He got quite good at that. It got to be a bit of a trend with Sammy over the next six to twelve months, and when we did ask him, he always had a good excuse to ward us off. It just became the norm for him to be out and about drinking. The main worry for us was that he seemed to be drinking in quite a few dodgy places, places I would never even think about going into. Not long after Daddy's 10th anniversary, Sammy got into a lot of trouble. He was on his own in a town where no Protestant in his right mind would go. It was full of nothing but IRA supporters and no doubt IRA men as well. Apparently, he walked in the front door brazen as hell, full drunk and out of his mind. He walked up to the bar, ordered a pint and slapped a pocket full of change on the bar. The barman leaned over at him. "I think you should turn around and walk back out the door you just came in."

In true Sammy fashion, he said. "Why, you are out of beer; not to worry, give me a gin and tonic and no ice 'cause it hurts my teeth."

"No, dummy. You're not welcome in here and my advice to you is to leave and do it now before someone in here sorts your teeth out for good and makes you leave. Too late boy, I did warn you." Last thing Sammy remembered was a click at his left ear. The hammer of a gun was pulled back and pointed at his ear. Speaking to a policeman who heard from a tout was that two men approached him, from each side, and pulled their guns on him. He got the butt of a gun to the back of the head and went out like a light. They give him a hell of a beating on the ground before he was dragged out back for the rest. The police found him dumped outside the town in a shuck. They didn't find out who he was until they got him to hospital and cleaned him up a bit. To this day, we never found out what he was doing there, but we can now guess. No one was ever arrested for the attack and never will because the RUC or army would never enter that town. If they did, there would be a blood bath. He took quite a beating that night and we hoped that it would be a turning point and he would change his ways. We were wrong. He just kept drinking. Sammy never had a family of his own because he could never hold down a relationship. With his looks, he never found it hard to get a girl, but it usually only lasted a few months or so. Week after week, he was getting drunk and ending up in strange places, and week after week, we ended up fetching him home. His work at the shop did suffer a bit but only because he would get there when he got out of bed from the night before. Mummy asked Alan to join the company to help out when it became difficult with Sammy's antics and he took to it well from day one. Sammy did begin to rely on him when he couldn't make it in on time which annoyed James no end and it got to the stage that they would come to blows over Sammy's time keeping and arriving at the shop smelling of drink and beat up. On a few occasions, the RUC landed at the door wanting to find out what Sammy was up to. Luckily enough, the same RUC man called each time and he just happened to be a friend of Daddy's back in their young days. He always spoke to Mummy alone. We knew he was trying to warn Sammy that he was on their radar because of reports getting to them. He didn't change his ways though he just tried to keep it low profile. Billy took over Sammy's job about two years into being there and Sammy went down to three or four days a week. Mummy or Uncle Alan would never get rid of him outright because he had a right to be there. It was so sad the way he was going but he had a lot to cope with on a personal level with all the pains and memories and he once told me that the drink become the only way to keep it all under control so he could see the day through. Fuck me, that poor bastard had a lot to go through, and it made us all so sad for him. Even though he and James had their differences, James would never see or hear a bad word against him, but he had the right as a loving brother to question his ways as we all did. The future was going to be very hard for Sammy, but the whole family had his back.

It's strange now when I think back to when Sammy would come home drunk, Mummy would never be angry with him, just worried about him. She never seemed to argue or shout at him and he would always explain himself to her when they were alone. Never once did she come to us asking us to step in and have a word though we could tell she was very worried. Sammy was on a personal journey and when we uncovered his journey in later years only then did we all understand and our love for him became stronger than ever.

Third Born

Stephen

Best place to start is from where I can remember. My life was full of ups and downs that ended up looking like a bloody yo-yo. I have some very vivid memories of Daddy and the time we had as a family. From an early age, I always wanted to be in the army and I put that down to seeing Daddy around the house in his uniform. I have memories of him putting his army cap on my head when he was leaving to go out on patrol. Mummy would lift me up and tell me to wave goodbye to Daddy and he would usually come over to kiss Mummy goodbye and put his cap on me. I couldn't wait as a wee cub for him to come home so I could get his cap. Mummy has some lovely photos of me with it on which take pride of place in my wallet next to my heart. Mummy used to refer to me as the wee middle man because I was born in the middle of six boys. That soon changed though when she had four more children. Richie would have been the middle man if he had lived. I didn't do as well as James and Sammy at school, as I knew what I wanted to do when I grew up. I joined the Boys Brigade (BB) as soon as I was old enough and loved every moment of it. We would go away on camps to Mourn Mountains or Gortin Glens and live off the land. Well, that's how we saw it, but they had everything in tins to be honest. Didn't matter; we loved it. One proud moment of mine was when we were camping over the weekend. A squad of UDR men just happened to be in the same area as us and they came over to speak to us. They were all camouflaged up and looked as scary as hell. Our BB leader told us that they wanted to talk to us about survival tips in the wild. He was in the UDR himself and arranged it all through his Commanding Officer (CO). When this large camouflage man stepped up to talk to us, I got the feeling that I knew his voice. It was my daddy. He talked for around ten minutes and answered some questions. My hand went up like a shot thinking he would pick me first. Well, he didn't. I got the last question. "Yes, young man, what's your question?"

"At what age did you want to join the army?"

His answer made my decision final. "It was around the same age as you are, cub." Through all the muck on his face, I could see him wink at me. I winked back, but I probably looked like I had an allergic reaction in my eye as I didn't know how to bloody wink. When they left, and we went back to our tents, I couldn't wait to tell the boys. The response was the same from everybody—a big 'wow'.

I was everybody's best friend in the BB from that point onwards. When it came to school lessons, Mummy pushed me as much as she did the other lads, but because I knew what I wanted to do, I fell short in the eleven plus and failed it. Daddy's death in my last year at primary school didn't help and Mummy put the fact that I did fail it down to that. Maybe it did but I just had to get on with it. Daddy's death hit me very badly and I needed to do things that kept me busy. In 1977, Mummy and Daddy got the chance to go away for a week to England where we had family. I was looked after by Aunty Sally and one Sunday she took me with her down to see her family in Fermanagh. I liked it so much, I asked to stay a while longer as it was during the summer holidays. Luckily, her mum liked me so much that she asked Mummy when she got back if I could stay for a few weeks, and Mummy said yes. It was the first of five years that I spent two or three weeks of the summer holidays there. Aunty Sally had a brother a couple of years older than me, and we got on like a house on fire. They lived on a big farm with lots of animals, but it was growing crops that they did most. I would be the first Richards at the lower school. Not a problem though as I had a lot of my BB friends at the same school and not only that the leader of the senior BB was a teacher there. He was also involved with the army cadets and I made it my mission to join up as soon as I could, but before I could, Mummy told me that if I wanted to join the cadets, I first had to show that I done well at school. My reports were so good that Mummy gave me permission to join the cadets, and on my first parade the whole family were there. I felt so proud of achieving the start of my dreams and follow in Daddy's footsteps. Mummy told me she was so proud of me and said she would support me in whatever I wanted to do in life. That was the army, but before I could join up, I had to show Mummy I was good enough to get good marks at school. One of my friends in the BB and at school was Andy Cobb. He lived in the same village and had gone through the same heartache as us. He lost two uncles, one killed by the INLA (Irish National Liberation Amy) and one killed by the IRA. I remember his uncle George and he was a kind and generous man. Andy had the same dreams as me and we would spend hours playing soldiers in the fields. The BB and Cadets were just a stepping stone to the full time army. When we finished school, we had only one thing in mind: get to Omagh and sign up, but first, we had to get our parents to sign the forms to allow us to do so. We decided to go to each of our parents together. Andy's family was first. His dad was okay with it as his family had a history within the forces. His mum, on the other hand, was dead against it. George was her brother. Andy stood up and shouted, "If you don't let me, Mum, I will wait till I can sign the papers myself and join up then. You won't stop me. I am joining up with or without your say so." His dad talked her around to say yes. That made it, one down and one to go. Now for my family. As we walked into the kitchen, most of the family were at the table eating. It was a Sunday evening.

"Mummy."

"Yes, Stephen?"

"I want your permission to join the army. Me and Andy want to join up together."

The kitchen was full of a deafening silence. James barked, "What the hell do you want to do that for, you idiot?"

"Be quiet, James." Mummy said. "I know this is what you have wanted all your life, Stephen, but I need to make sure you make the right decision. This is your whole life you're signing up for."

"Ever since I was a toddler, Mummy, you know this is all I ever wanted." I grabbed my school bag and pulled out my picture of me wearing Daddy's UDR cap. "You know this is what I want to do, Mummy. It's not just about Daddy's death, and no, I haven't forgotten our promise to him either. Please, Mummy, please." She looked at all us boys around the table, then looked over at a photo of Daddy on the wall before nodding her head yes. I ran over and gave her a big hug and kiss before running outside with Andy. We roared with happiness as we cycled down the lane. The next day we took our signed forms down to Omagh and signed our futures over to the army.

The moment we had talked about for most of our young lives was one step away. Six weeks later, that last step was upon us. Both our whole families were there to see us off in Omagh and they were both overjoyed for us and also so upset that we would be leaving home for the first time. Mummy took me aside and hugged me so tight. I will never forget her words to me and the way she said them as she fixed my hair. "My wee middle man, what am I going to do without you around the house? Please promise me you'll be good and do the right thing 'cause your daddy will be watching over you. He always said you were a soldier in the making and that we would always give you our full support." She hugged and kissed me again and said, "Don't forget your daddy," then just turned and walked away. My brothers then said goodbye to me in turn and said the same thing to me. One thing for sure, I didn't need reminding. On the way in, we forgot to look back; we were that excited, but they didn't mind and I'm sure they had a laugh about it. The first weeks of training went well for us because we spent so much time in the BB and cadets. We understood what an order was and how to accept it. We both wanted to join the Royal Marines and never changed our minds. Training was hard. The Royal Marines has the longest infantry training, which is 32 weeks. That's for new recruits and it has to be when they are turning civilians into commandos. For us to wear that Green Beret, we had to pass the commando test, the final one being a 30-mile march. We had to have a high standard of fitness because our bodies would be broken by months of unrelenting military training. We could only pass these tests with balls, grit and mental fortitude. Places like Dartmoor and the Brecon Beacons were not to be taken likely. We lost a comrade on the mountains during our training which brought us back down to earth with a bang. Our CO (Commanding Officer) took us all aside and laid it out for us to see. As he read us the riot act, the lad we lost was taken to a waiting ambulance in front of us. "That's the result of someone in over their heads and got cocky. If you think it won't happen to you, you're fucking next. Well, no more on my watch. If you think you're not fucking up to it feel free to fuck off and die somewhere else." It was very harsh, but in our world, it is real life and not some shit TV show. That night in the mess we all got sloshed because the next day was a down day. Andy and I talked over what had happened and assured each other that we had each other's backs. Two weeks later was the big test—a 30-mile fully equipped march. This is a march across the dreaded Dartmoor which you will need to complete in less than eight hours, of course, carrying your rifle and equipment. It was so fucking hard, but we knew that. We never took it lightly and trained for the last year to get to this point. During the march we pushed and pushed each other to the end and there was no way this fucking bog was going to deny us. We finished together well within the eight hours. We were two young eighteen-year-old boys from Ulster taking on one of the most dangerous environments on earth and we won.

We began our lives as Royal Marine Commandos at the age of 18 in late 1987. We both passed with flying colours, but Andy was not too happy. He was told that because he was from Northern Ireland he would not be stationed there under any circumstances, well, barring a civil war, that is. It would have been too dangerous to send someone from there to serve as he would most likely be recognised. The main reason Andy joined up was so that he could hunt for the men who killed two of his uncles. I always knew that was his reason and to an extent it was one of my reasons as well. I knew I could do more to find out info in the army but it was also my dream. He did, though, get his head down and learn to become the best soldier he could. We spent the next year or so travelling around the world not only training but being sent into war torn areas to do peace-keeping duties and that was even though a war was still going on back home. Operation Banner was ongoing in Ulster and was so until 2007. It was and still is the longest continuous deployment in the British military's history and in some people's minds it should still be in operation. 1969–2007. The first time we went into a war-torn area was in Kosovo. The Kosovo War started in late February 1998 and lasted until 11 June 1999. It was fought by the forces of the Federal Republic of Yugoslavia and the Kosovo Albanian rebel group known as the Kosovo Liberation Army (KLA). It was a goddamn bloody cluster fuckup which we should have steered clear of but when NATO called, the British were seen to always shout, "Here we are." We both spent a couple of months there but never fired a shot. I did see my first war dead though and it stopped me in my tracks. We came across a young boy who was about the same age as our Boyd crumbled in a heap with his legs blown off. His eyes were wide open looking to the sky. The hard thing to understand was no one picked him up and buried him. I was to find out later that the rest of his family were also dead and at the back of the house in a freshly dug pit. They were made to dig their own graves before being shot kneeling in the hole.

Not a nice baptism of fire for us. It was the first and would not be the last body we came across. I didn't get to go home much as it was too dangerous for me back home. The fact that our family was targeted before would make it quite a queue if the IRA where to kill the son of a UDR man they had already killed. I did, however, sneak home a few times to see the family but stayed on the farm the whole time. I was flown in by chinook to Belfast and then picked up by one of the brothers. It was always great to see everyone, especially Mummy. The second time I got home I spent some time with Sammy and it worried me that he was hitting the drink very hard. I tried to help him but unless he admitted he had a problem, he couldn't be helped. The day I was leaving, he called home to say goodbye. He gave me a letter and told me to only open it when I got back to the barracks. I told him I was only a phone call away, and no matter the day or time, if he needed me, just call me. That letter sayed in my pocket until I got to the barracks. When I opened it it turned out to be typical Sammy. "Don't worry about me you gobshit. Look after your self and don't get shot in the bollax. HaHa, Seriously Stephen, Please stay safe bro, some day you will understand me. Love you lad, Sammy" Not often do I laugh and cry at the same time, but this was one of them. In 1990, we would see our first action on the battlefield. The Gulf war had begun when the Iraqi army invaded Kuwait. We were sent out in the second wave and initially we were not supposed to be on the front line but some plans didn't work out and we had to handle the retreating army of Saddam Hussein because they got destroyed within a few months. It was a 'Hold the line' order and let no one through. At the beginning of February in 1991, we came under fire from retreating Iraqi soldiers. It was during the night and was so unexpected because we had no Intel on movement in our area. There were about twenty to thirty men, all on foot, who attacked the edge of our line and it was more like a run for freedom rather than attack the line. They came at us out of the dark in force and they were cut down in minutes. It was hand to hand in some areas which is what we were trained for and they didn't stand a chance. We had night scopes on and knew where our booby traps were. This is the battle where I had my first kill and one I would remember. I was on the Radio comms getting updates when he came my way not knowing I was there. I caught him with a blow to the head as he passed, and he went down, as I approached him he pulled a knife on me. I blocked his swinging arm, unarmed him and used his own knife to take him out just as I was trained. Not thinking about it, I just looked to my front again ready to defend the line. It was all over in about ten minutes. When daylight came, we checked for our casualties, which there were none, then we checked for Iraqi dead or wounded. I made my way over to the Iraqi that I got, and yep, he was dead. He looked scruffy and looked like he hadn't eaten in days but better him than me. I thought it would feel different taking a man's life, but it felt like job well done to me. It was my first kill but would not be the last. The Gulf war only lasted for about five months with victory for the coalition forces, Kuwait was free again and Saddam had his ass handed to him on a platter. Why the fuck he got to stay in power is beyond me. He should have been dealt with there and then because three years later we had to go in again and this time it would last for quite some time. This time the fucker was caught, tried and sentenced to death. Saddam Hussein was hung on 30th December 2006. Five years too fuckin' late though. The Royal Marines were heavily involved in the second conflict and took some losses. I spent a total of fourteen months in Iraq during the Operation Iraqi freedom. That's what the Yanks called it and it kind of stuck. I killed upward of ten Iraqi soldiers this time around and it was most likely more because we used booby traps that they left for us. We didn't hang around to count the dead. Andy was also involved but he was attached to another company. We met up a few times, and I can tell you it was good to see an old friend. We talked through the night about the battles and as I knew he would, Andy was in the thick of it. He was promoted to lieutenant because of his decisions in the face of battle and I was now at the rank of sergeant. He was always an officer in the making, that boy, and on one of the last occasions we caught up the war was still in full flow, he said he had something to tell me. I wasn't worried, but it took me by surprise. I always knew he wanted to go to the top. "Something I need to tell you, lad. I have been working towards this since we joined the Marines some twelve years ago. I've put myself forward for the SAS (Special Air Service) selection and it's been accepted. I'm off back to the UK in two weeks." I didn't expect him to go that high, but the SAS is the highest and the best in the British Army.

"Are you fucking nuts, Andy? What are you thinking, fella? Trying to get into that shit could fuckin' kill you. Our selection for the Royals was a cake walk compared to that hell. Why? Wait, don't tell me 'cause I fucking know why. Listen Andy, you will never step foot back in Ulster in active service even with the SAS."

He looked at me as if to say little do you know sunshine. "I've been speaking to some of the boys from D squadron and they said I would be okay and to go for it. Whether or not I get back into Ulster is something I can work on and anyway it's what I want no matter if I do or if I don't."

"Fuck me, Andy, are you sure about this 'cause being returned to unit (RTU) if you fail is not good. You will be known as a failure to some."

"Fuck them, lad, I don't give a shit about them cunts and if I do, which I won't, I will try again." It all went quite for a few moments as we calmed down. I pulled a bottle of Bushmills from my pocket, poured two drinks and handed him one.

"Listen, Andy, you're like my brother and I will always have your back no matter what, no matter what." We toasted, downed it in one and finished the bottle. Next time I saw Andy, he was a member of 22 SAS Regiment. During my time in the army, I got married to an English girl called Mary and we had one child, a little girl called Rosie, born in 1999. Mary was a great girl and a great mum, but because of my job, it just didn't work out. It only lasted four years and out of the four years of marriage I spent more time with the army than I did at home with Mary. We split on good terms. Mummy did get to see my family on a couple of occasions, but she had to visit us in England because of security risks. She had yet another granddaughter to spoil, but visits to us were few and far between. When the turn of the century came, I was on active service in Iraq and never even noticed it coming or going. The one thing I had to do was to call Mummy and the brothers which wasn't easy. I eventually got the chance and wished them all a happy new year. Sammy was not there and couldn't be found. He was now a full-on alcoholic and driving everyone to despair. Something needed to be done or he would kill himself.

Fourth Born

Billy

Billy was the fourth born to the family. He was born in 1970 and was nine years old when Daddy was killed. He, like Sammy, was in the car when Daddy was attacked and killed. He never got shot but was badly cut up by glass and metal fragments due to the furiousness of the bullets that hit the car. He was pushed under the dash in the passenger's side by Daddy when it started and luckily for him the engine block was his bullet proof vest. Being the last person on this earth to see Daddy alive and to have looked into his eyes until the moment he died was a burden that no one should ever have to go through, let alone a nine-year-old boy. One of the only times he did talk to me about it we were in our teens sitting in the barn cleaning the grey Fergie for a show. Just me and Billy. I felt so sorry for him. When he was under that dash, he was fixated on Daddy's eyes watching his life drain away. He held his hand until Uncle Sam arrived on the scene. I can't imagine having to go through that.

"When they got me out of the car, I didn't want to let go of his hand, Stephen, because the warmth of Daddy's hand on that cold morning was still there. I could feel the blood running onto my hand as he grew weaker. I just didn't want to let go. When Aunty June lifted me out of the car and put me in her car, she left me to go back to Daddy. I felt so alone. I could hear them all shouting at Daddy not to give up. Uncle

106

Sam began to scream as loud as he could, 'No, no, come on, William, talk to me, come on, lad.' It was no good, Stephen, he took too many hits. That last shot to the head by the cunt that walked up to the car did it. That's what sticks in my mind the most, Stephen. The look in that bastard's eyes as he grinned at me with happiness in what they just did". Billy leaned over to me and whispered, "I intend to look into those eyes again someday and watch that cunt's life drain away and I will make sure I let him know that just before I send him straight to hell." My God, he meant it as well. "When I was put in that car alone, I looked at my hands and Daddy's blood was still wet in the palm of my right hand. I tried to rub it off, but I had blood everywhere by then. Next thing I know some woman was praying for me." All that Daddy kept saying to Billy right up to the end of his life was, "It will be all right Billy." It traumatized him for a long time, and after a year or so, he would never talk of it unless he felt like he had to. We will never know the heavy burden he felt knowing he was the last person Daddy looked at, and for those first years after the death, he was a very quiet boy. He kept to himself usually in his bedroom and didn't really get involved in conversation that much.

His schooling did suffer a lot for him especially when he was taking his eleven plus the following year. He ended up failing it and joining me at the lower school in Omagh. I was glad to have another brother with me at school and I knew he would be okay unlike James and Sammy who faced ignorance about Mummy's religion at their school. Mummy took me aside before his first day at school and asked me to look after him and not to let anyone pick on him, which I would have done anyway. The hard thing that Billy had to deal with was that Daddy's death was still very raw when he started a new school. I did my best but sometimes it wasn't good enough and the only thing that did help was to let him go home early from school to be with Mummy on the farm. He seemed to be calm and okay on the farm but then it helped every one of us when we felt down. For me, it always felt like the animals wouldn't let you down and gave us something to focus on. His first year at school was not good for him and he fell short on his lessons; he did, however, take to sports and loved playing rugby and football. After about a year at school, he settled down and eventually caught up with the other children in his year. He started to excel in nearly every class and began to come out of his shell a bit. He joined the BB with me and joined in with everything we did. He still had the love for rugby and we all noticed the he was starting to fill out a bit and began to look like a very fit young man. From what I remember, he only had one incident at school when some little prick tried to belittle him in front of the class. He waited until his class had a PE class and it was a double period on that day and it just happened to be rugby. That little prick got mullered for fifty minutes and ended up going to A&E to be checked over. He didn't speak to him; he just looked in his eyes every time he got the hit in. Billy left his mark on nearly every part of his body. When he told us, he just said, "Job done, prick sorted." That was when we knew he was going to be a handful for any man in a fight. Round about 1985, when he was fifteen, he began to show signs of wanting to be more true to his religion. He joined a flute band and started to show his support for Rangers football club; now, you might think there was nothing wrong with that but he become very loyal. I didn't see a problem in it but James and Mummy did. I suppose the fact that James was the oldest, he tried to show him better ways to go. It didn't work. He didn't fall out with us or fight with us; he just made his point very strongly that he loved his country and was sick of the Provos murdering Protestant people. There was no doubt that once he joined the flute band, influences took a bearing on his decisions. I remember one year the 12th July parade was in the Cross and Billy's band were marching. He would make sure that whenever they were outside a well-known pub the band would slow to a stop and play as loud as they could. He wanted to make sure that the owners got the point of their actions. He was on such a high that day and would talk about it for days after. We were proud of him and he loved it, but the ethos of the band was more Loyalist than Unionist. A

Loyalist would lean more towards the paramilitary's than a Unionist would. One incident that drove him more toward hard-line loyalism was that two of the band members were killed by the IRA. That turned him against every Catholic, whether they are decent people who hated the IRA or the opposite. That was the turning point for him that made him cross over that line, yet he would always show the upmost respect for the family and never let his beliefs cloud his judgement about family. To Mummy's displeasure, Billy decided that he didn't want to go into further education after school. He said there was nothing in it for him, but luckily for us, Uncle Alan spent some time with him and he changed his mind. He got him to go into further education and learn a trade. He would become an engineer just like Sammy and eventually take over that position. Going to the Tec kind of helped him change his views on Catholics. He was around them every day and got to make some friends, not close friends, but just friends he could talk to on a daily basis. He did well at Tec and, like James and Sammy, passed with flying colours. He stepped right into the job at the shop and worked under Uncle Alan. He was good at his job and had no issues dealing with both Catholic and Protestants on the shop floor. You would never have known that a few years earlier he would have spit in a Catholic's face rather than speak to them; now he speaks to them as you would a friend. Not long after Billy started in the shop, he had a visitor that caught James's attention. It was James Wright, a cousin to Daddy and also a member of the UVF. He spent half an hour in the office with Billy talking and seemed very friendly. James remembered what he had said to us at the funeral and was concerned that Billy had contacted him during his wayward days and he had got himself into something very dangerous. The next time I got the chance to speak to Billy I brought it up. He told me straight that he had enough of waiting on the RUC to find Daddy's killers and he was going to do the job himself. He promised me that he had not joined the UVF or UDA (Ulster Defence Association) and had no intentions in doing so. Apparently, all he was doing was getting advice from Jimmy.

"Listen, Billy, you need to sort yourself out here. When dealing with these fuckers you need to stay unknown and not be seen to mouth off at every goddamn thing that the Provo's do. You will put yourself on their radar and you won't be able to turn left without them knowing; not only that, lad, the police will be doing the same bloody thing. Stay below the radar and unknown to them. That way you can watch them, gather intel and be ready to get the bastards. That's exactly what them cunts are doing to us so make friends with them, get them to like you and work from within. Get to know your enemy." From a soldier's point of view, that's sound advice and exactly what I would do, though I was worried that he would get in so deep he would never be able to get out. We hoped that Billy would settle down when he met a girl from Londonderry and started to have a family. They bought a house outside the Cross next to the home farm so Mummy had a chance to be in their lives and help out when needed. She loved having her family around her. He never married Heather, but they had two beautiful children—a boy called William after Grandad D and a girl called Ruth. Heather was from a family of true loyalists and was of the same opinion as Billy so to say they got on together was an understatement. She had lost an Uncle who was a member of the RUC killed by the IRA and a cousin who was a member of the UVF killed while trying to plant a bomb under the car of a local Sinn Fein councillor. He wouldn't have any arguments about his stance at home that's for sure. They were good together and always looked like a happy family. His two wonderful children would go to the same school as we did, and they had plenty of cousins around them at school. Knowing Billy as we did, we all thought he would join the UDR to get the answers we needed to find out who was behind Daddy's death, but he didn't. He did, however, have a serious amount of friends in both the UDR and RUC, and without question, he was getting info from someone about who was doing what around the Tyrone area. That was obvious because of the numbers of IRA and INLA killers being taken out in by UVF or UDA gangs. They would have needed help. As I said, we didn't know for sure what or if Billy was involved in, but James had a very late visit from a family friend who was also in the RUC and off duty one evening that worried us greatly. He was the same RUC man at Daddy's funeral that spoke to us.

"I don't know the best way to put this James, so I'm going to put it to you straight. We are watching Billy. Reports are, and they are reliable reports if you get my meaning, that he's heavily involved in UVF activities around here." How do you know that he asked him?

"What proof do you have, Alan? You just can't come here and spurt out something like that and expect me to fuckin' take you seriously. Now you just said to me that you were just going to put it straight; well, I want it straight. What the fuck do you mean when you say reliable reports?" The look on his face was enough to make James think that this was serious.

"Right; you didn't hear this from me, James and I will deny everything and have you fucking arrested if this comes back at me and bites me in the arse. There's a mole in the UVF and he's singing like a fuckin bird to save his own ass. He's saying that Billy is the main man in this area and directs everything that happens. Nothing and I mean nothing happens without his say. It's very fucking serious, James, and I can't emphasise that enough. Plans are afoot to bring him in for questioning."

He got up to leave before turning to me and saying, "Warn him that we will be calling for him but for fuck's sake don't tell him about what I told you, James, 'cause if it's true you know what could happen. Just tell him to play along because we have no proof at the moment but understand me, they will find proof if it's out there." They shook hands and he left. James told Billy he needed a hand and to call at the home farm the next day, which he did. When he told him everything that Alan had said it was like he knew right away who it was that was talking to the RUC. He just kept his cool and told James not to worry that he would sort it out. James wasn't stupid and knew exactly what he meant. As he left the barn, James begged him to be careful because Mummy would never get over losing another one.

"Don't you worry, James, I would never do anything to upset Mummy."

Two days later, Alan was back and this time in uniform. "You told him didn't you, James. You just couldn't hold on until we had a chat with him could you. It might have been all lies and nothing to worry about for fuck's sake but now questions are being asked of me to find out who within the RUC talked. Shit and fan comes to mind. We will be coming with guns drawn now, James, so if anything goes wrong it's on you and not me." No handshakes this time. Sure enough, that evening at his home Billy was taken in for questioning. He was in for three days straight with no one but his solicitor allowed visiting. He was released without charge as he had a solid alibi for the evening the tout was killed. Needless to say, the rest of the accusations went away so to speak because there was no one to substantiate the claims; however, the RUC would now know about Billy and watch him closely. According to what we were told, the UVF man who touted on Billy was an idiot but had close ties to UVF command in Belfast. Nothing more happened about his death because it was put down to an IRA attack. Somehow, the UVF got a hold of an IRA gun that was linked to the murders of security force members all over Ulster and used it to make it look like that the IRA did it. Well, it worked, because forensics come back that it was indeed an IRA gun that was used to kill him, and the IRA got blamed.

Billy became very smart and intelligent from that point and became very powerful at mind games. No one would be allowed to know what he did or was about to do and I could see that nearly everything he did was thought through to the last detail. He did what he had to do without anyone knowing and that's including Mummy or the brothers. We will never know the whole extent of his actions, because he was the sort of man that would take it to his grave. The name lone-wolf comes to mind with Billy.

Fifth Born

John

John was the sixth boy born in our family but because baby Richie, who was the fifth born, died at birth, John would always be known as the fifth boy. John was five years old at the time of Daddy's shooting and has very little memories of Daddy at all. He can associate memories of Daddy with things like the tractors or with Root the dog but mostly it's with Daddy in his army uniform. He remembers him getting ready for his shifts and some of us boys always arguing about who gets to clean his guns or clean his boots when he returned. Sometimes, Daddy would take off his boots and give one boot to John and the other boot to the one whose turn it was to clean them. It usually ended up with that cub doing both the boots anyway. At five, he wasn't that good at it, but he thought it was great that Daddy would think to give him a chance. Whenever we would talk about Daddy as a group, John would always tell the few stories he could only remember. We never got fed up with them because the memories were precious to him and that's all that mattered. Because John like Boyd didn't have a father figure, it was difficult for him to stand up for himself and stand his ground. He did rely on us older boys to step in and back him up if he needed it, but that wasn't too often, thank God. He was always a very calm and relaxed lad who never gave Mummy any concerns. There was no doubt he got that from the church. He became an avid church-goer at a very early age and it was through being in the BB. The junior BB had a vicar as the adjutant who was second to the captain and he used his position to make sure all the boys were well-versed in the Bible scripters. That was by no means a bad thing, as he was not one to ram it down your throats if you didn't like it. John just happened to take to it. He did well at primary school, passed his eleven plus and joined James and Sammy in going to the upper school in Omagh. They had both left by then, so John was going to be there on his own just like I was when I went to the lower school. That was in 1985 and the troubles were in full flow with people still losing their lives in every corner of Ulster. He, unlike us older boys, had no trouble whatsoever at school. By that stage, children of his age knew nothing of Mummy's religion or Daddy's death. He never spoke about it unless he was asked to. If he knew you, he would engage in conversion about it, but if he didn't, he would stay clear of it. He became an integral part of the BB, joining the seniors and rose through the ranks to become a lieutenant. He would take over from the adjutant when he was not available and became quite good at giving the religious services on Sundays. Through the years of his service, he never once missed a BB night or event. He loved working with the young people and spreading the word of God to who ever wanted to join. Mummy once sent me a paper clipping of John with the BB and with a special guest—the big man himself, the Reverend Ian Paisley. He was congratulating him on his promotion within the Church and the BB. My God, did he live on the photo for a long time. He used to say, "Big Ian and me are so tight, he has my phone number on speed dial." I would say John most likely does have big Ian's number somewhere. John ended up going to University in Belfast to Mummy's delight and she would bring it up whenever she could. Having one of her boys at University was a big deal for her and I would say two fingers up to Granny D. Not a soul in the Cross didn't know and most likely hoped that Boyd didn't follow him. Imagine Mummy telling all about having two sons at Uni. He was very intelligent and spoke well, which led him to become speaker of debates at school and he relished the post. I remember Mummy telling us that one evening she attended a university event with a guest speaker where John led the evening. She couldn't believe that he could speak so well and in front of nearly 300 people. She always thought he was a shy lad. Well he was, but with this sort of thing, he was in his element. During his time at uni, he met a gorgeous girl who suited him down to earth. She was at one of his speaker nights when she asked him a question that he had no answer for. When we would ask about being battered by a girl, he always said, "I knew that someday she would be my wife, so I knew not to argue or talk back. I learned quickly." Grace was a Christian girl from a good Unionist family in the heartland of Portadown. He couldn't have picked better if he tried, but then again, she picked him. He spent three years in Belfast studying before coming back to the Cross and becoming a teacher of History and RE (Religious Education) at the upper school in Omagh. He kept seeing Grace, his girlfriend, but it was a bit of a long-distance relationship. He would travel up every other weekend and Grace would do the same. It worked for them, and in the summer of 1996, they got married in Portadown. I never made it over for the wedding because I was deployed but my wife Mary did. She spent three weeks with Mummy and got on well with everyone in our family; also, she became very close friends with John's new wife Grace. Grace and Mary spent a lot of time together which suited me and John. Years later, when my Mary was giving birth, Grace was by her side and become our daughter Rosie's Godmother. Just before Rosie was born, Grace and John announced they were having their third baby. It would be the third of four children for them. They had two boys and two girls. They settled down in the outskirts of Portadown where John started teaching in a local college. Life was good for him with a large family around him. The troubles where still raging all around us when it made its mark on us once again. John and Grace were to be hit with a hammer blow to their world. Grace's mum and dad were involved in a car accident when the police were in pursuit of a stolen car after it was involved in an unsuccessful shooting of a RUC man in Belfast. The stolen car hit Grace's parent's car as they were making their way home from visiting the grandkids. They didn't stand a chance. They were killed four weeks before the birth of their fourth grandchild. I did get over to see the family on compassionate leave, to give John some moral support, and fuck me, he needed it. The poor lad was in bits not only with the loss, but he was at a crossroads with his faith, not being able to understand why God would let him down so much. All us boys rallied around them for support and also support for Mummy. Yet again, she had to handle grief at the hands of terrorism. It all flooded back to her having to go to the funerals of two victims of IRA terrorism.

Even though it wasn't a direct attack on them, the result of their actions caused the crash which resulted in their deaths. The day of the funeral we stood shoulder to shoulder as a family knowing what to expect for John and Grace. Grace was the only child which left her with no one to turn to but John. He had to be there every moment for her and we had no doubt he would. We just made sure we were there for him if he needed us. During this troubled time for John, he would talk to us about Daddy and the fact that he had doubts about his faith, so one night as we all sat round the family table, we encouraged him to get everything off his chest. He cried and prayed, then prayed and cried, and not once did we lose sight of his pain. That night when he had his final say, Sammy turned to him and said, "You are the rock and backbone of this family, John. You never lost sight of what helped you through which in turn helped us in a way. You might not have known it, but we envied you for the path you took in life and the way that path helped you. I would give anything and everything, as I'm sure the others would, to be able to turn to a faith that would clear a path for us to bring peace in our lives, but I don't. I have a demon eating at me from the inside and I don't have that faith to clear my path ahead and rid it from inside me. You do, lad. Because of you, that girl and those children will understand why this happened and believe that God had a different road for them. If you give up, they will give up and your journey in life will not be in your or God's hands."

We all were in tears because of what Sammy said. It was from the heart, and what Sammy was going through, he showed that he had never lost that love we have for each other. John got up off of his seat, walked over to us, put his hand on Sammy's shoulder and started to pray.

"Dear Lord. I thank you that you love my dear brothers as much if not more than I do, and I pray that the joy of the Lord will be their strength, as it was for me in my time of need. Thank you, Lord, for loving us so much, amen." What Sammy said that night gave John his faith back and also helped him deal with what he had on the road ahead. Sammy, on the other hand, give us all belief that he could beat the demons he had in his life. I only wish that Sammy could have listened to the words that he said that night because now he needed them more than John did. It was not going to be easy for Grace in the coming months but with the help of us all, they would come through. From that moment onwards, John become the man that we all knew he was again. After the birth of their fourth child, they took life day by day and grew stronger and stronger. He became the deputy head of the school he worked in and Grace become a great mother to four great children. The loss was not forgotten by them but through their faith and time they come through. John was always there for Sammy when he needed him, and Sammy would always confide in John. That was the only way we truly knew what Sammy was up to.

Sixth Born

Boyd

Boyd was the last of the boys born and he was three years old when Daddy died. It's very sad knowing that Boyd has no memories of Daddy at all. He often said that it was not fair that we all had memories and he didn't. The only thing he has are photographs that Mummy gathered up over the years. Nearly every photo that Mummy had of Daddy was put up on his bedroom wall as a reminder of what he looked like. If anyone came across a photo of Daddy, they would always let Boyd have a copy and Boyd would go to bed at night hoping he would have a dream or a memory of his own someday. It just never happened. Sometimes, he would get very angry when we would start talking about Daddy in his company and start shouting at us to shut up about Daddy, and then other times he would ask us to tell more stories because it made him feel happy. It would all depend on how he felt at that given time, so we would only tell funny or happy stories in his presence so not to upset him. One thing is for sure; he always got the best care and attention from Mummy and anyone who visited the farm when he was younger. They would always spoil him rotten and Uncle Mickey was the person who always give him a lot of attention with the usual sweets. John did get the same attention, but Boyd was, without doubt, the spoilt one of the family. He didn't, however, go through the same pain as we did, because it was all so raw in our hearts and minds. We cried and cried for what felt like years, whereas Boyd and John had very little or no memories to cry over. Don't get me wrong; they did go through some very bad times as they got older because the whole family suffered together. Something happened to Boyd when he was fourteen that brought him down to earth with a bang. He worked at the weekends and days off with a local builder labouring for him. He enjoyed it and he got to save more money for his future. One morning when he got to Mr Graham's house he was asked if he would go up an old tree to remove a tri-colour put up overnight. It was down the road a bit from his house and it annoyed him. Usually when you see a tri-colour like that it means it's a Republican's only area. Boyd said no problem and as they got to the tree, he got out of the van to take it down. Just as he got to the grass verge, Mr Graham shouted for him to come back as there was a car coming. They planned to get it down on the way back from the day's work. On the way back, the road to his house was cordoned off by the RUC and when he asked why he was informed that a British soldier went up a tree to remove a tri-colour and it blew up as he did. The soldier lost both of his arms. That would put the shit up the hardest of men, let alone a young boy. Boyd didn't let it get to him but there is no doubt it made him think twice about doing such things. He was a very funny lad with a great temperament, but if you annoyed him badly, he could be a very nasty little shit. When I left for the Army he was only a ten-year-old boy and I remember him crying that I was going away. That changed after a few years and when I did get home on leave, the first thing he would say to me when I got home was, "What do you want? You don't live here so you don't." That was the beginning of the dreaded teen years that all parents and older siblings had nightmares about. Well, he was that nightmare to me. After a few hours of being home, he got used to it and became that funny lad again. It was like an alpha male tiger encroaching on another alpha male's territory and only when the tiger realises he's not a threat he backs down, and of course if you bribe him a gift. He did well at primary school and went on to pass his eleven plus and got to go to the same school as James, Sammy and John went to. With Billy at the Technical College, John was the only one of us left still at school and would help Boyd out if he ever needed it, but it didn't take long for him to make his mark and fit in at the school. He was never in bother or never had any issues at school. He just seemed to get on with it. He eventually ended up going to the Tec like all the other lads except me. He studied business and a host of courses to do with the building trade. Two years later, he joined a local building company and began his working life. Within six months, he had become an office manager and had over sixty people working under him on different building sites and in different offices. He was beginning to become a very intelligent young man. Looking back to when he was starting his teen years, there one thing Boyd did do, however that upset us a little. He decided that Daddy's old grey Fergie was now his and no one would take it off him. He was only twelve for fuck's sake and he was demanding that the tractor was now his. Seriously? The arguments that he had with the boys about it would lead to shouting matches that would be heard for miles. There was no talking to him. He wanted the tractor, end of story. Mummy was very upset about the arguing and to keep him quiet and to keep the peace she told him that when he reached his 18th birthday he could have the Grey, but it was always going to be the farm tractor and that the work on the farm came first. He agreed and, to his credit, he said he wouldn't have it any other way, so the grey Fergie would become his when he turned eighteen. He saved nearly every bit of his pocket money for that tractor, and when he turned eighteen, he spent it all on the Grey just to keep it looking like it was the day Daddy died, and what a great job he made of it. He took the photos he had of Daddy on the tractor down off his bedroom walls and put them in a large photo frame to hang in the tractor shed. He would use them to restore it to its former glory. It wasn't in that bad a condition even though it was used on a daily basis on the farm; it was that Boyd wanted to make his own stamp on it and to restore the Grey as Daddy did in the seventies. Uncle Alan give us an old Massy Fergusson to help us out while Boyd worked on the Grey so as not to cause problems on the farm. The day he finished restoring the Grey, he unveiled it like it was the unveiling of the Titanic itself. As I said, he was a funny bugger at times and could make the dead laugh. He got himself a PA system and wired it up in the shed and as he drove the Grey out of the shed for the first time he had Steppenwolf's 'Born to be Wild' blasting out like hell. I wasn't there but according to Sammy, who was videoing the whole thing, it was hilarious but at the same time fantastic. I got a copy of the video a few months later and played it to the lads at camp. The funniest comment to come from the lads when I showed it was, "Look at that mad fucker go. He's a Richards, all right." It did make me homesick for the farm though. Before long, he would start taking it to shows just like Daddy did, and whenever he entered it into a show, it was always entered as Owner—William Richards. The one trophy that he always wanted to win was at the Tyrone classic and cultural show. It was The William Richards Memorial Cup. Grandad D dedicated the cup to his memory back in 1982 for the best tractor in show. People from all over the island entered their tractors in the Tyrone show and winners come from all over, north and south. Grandad D didn't enter his own tractor in the first few years because he wanted the trophy to go far and wide, so everyone knew who it was for. It became the must win trophy for all classic tractor owners. I remember well the 1986 show when a lovely old man from Donegal won it for the first time and Sammy aged nineteen presented him with the trophy. The old man started to cry when he received the trophy and gave a very touching speech.

"For all of you who don't know me, I got to know this young gentleman back in the late 1970s. He helped me out many a time when I needed some advice. He actually called at my house in Donegal once with George to lend a hand. That was some help that young man gave me. I never forgot all his help and on the day he was killed I cried with shame. I was ashamed to be an Irishman and I have never gotten over it to this day. This is the proudest day of my life to receive William's trophy. Thank you and may God bless William and his family." That's why Boyd wanted to win the trophy, because of the standing Daddy had in the classic surroundings. In 1996, Boyd entered the Grey into that very category. He spent every evening and weekend he could to get it ready for its first show. The moment he drove into the arena everyone there knew that there was only one winner. Judges from all over the island were unanimous in their votes. And that year Mummy picked Uncle Alan to present the trophy to the winner and to our delight the classic club judges picked Daddy's Grey Fergie as winner. Boyd was over the moon and he deserved all the accolades coming to him. There was a lot of tears that day from Daddy's friends. Uncle Alan was so delighted for him, he asked if he could put the Grey Fergie in the shop showroom with the trophy. The Grey made it into so many magazines and papers and the headlines were so nice to see. "The little Grey is back." It was now famous. It stayed at the shop for a couple of weeks before Mummy asked for it back to do some work on the farm. Uncle Alan offered to give Mummy his Massy for good just to keep the Grey on show for a while longer, but famous or not it had a job to do. They settled for another two weeks, but after that, it was back to work for the Grey. Boyd didn't enter into that category again, but he did every other one that he could. Credit where credit is due. He made us all proud. As Boyd got older, he matured into a fine young man who made Mummy very proud. He was now a manager of a very large company who had a large work force but before long he decided he wanted to be his own boss. He spent three years with that company and learned a lot about the business. In 2001, at the age of 25, he started his own company. It would progress to a very well-known small building company that was growing each year. He met a girl at an end of year party one night who ended up being his wife. She was the daughter of a well-known UUP (Ulster Unionist Party) minister in Tyrone. Her name was Georgina, and she was a nurse at the local hospital. They got on like a house on fire and within two years of meeting they married. Boyd, like the lad he is, proposed to her the old way by first asking her father for permission to marry his daughter. I think Georgina's father was surprised by this and give him his permission to do so but only after asking him what plans he had for the future, so he could look after his daughter. Boyd's plans for his own company meant he was welcomed with open arms into the family. At the beginning of the year 2000, Boyd and Georgina got married. Boyd asked Sammy to be his best man at the wedding and just as he had done before, Sammy stepped up and become the man we all knew he could be. He would never let the family down at such an event. Mummy again was so happy to see one of her sons bring another daughter into the family. He was the last of us boys to get married and start a family. Within the year, Georgina got pregnant with their first child. They ended up with three children. They had two boys and a girl. After the third child, they both said that that three was more than enough. Boyd decided to buy some land adjacent to the home farm and within a year had built a house for his new family. He also built his company's offices and workshop on the land which meant the area was fast becoming homestead for the Richards family. James, Alan and Boyd all live on the farm land or next to it with Sammy still living in the old home. Only John and I lived away from home, but our hearts would always be at home on the farm.

Chapter 8
Time to Remember

At a time where our family seemed to be in a place of happiness, we all looked forward to Christmas and the New Year and what it would bring for us as a family. It was coming to the end of 2002 and Mummy had grandchildren on every corner of the family farm. When she walked out her front door, no matter what way she looked or turned, she would see one of her son's homes and in each home was a happy family with the laughter of children. James who lived on the edge of the farm to her left had three children, two girls and one boy. Billy, who lived on the other side of the land to her right, had two children, a boy and a girl and Boyd who had three children, two boys and one girl, had a large house and business right in front of her as she walked out the back door. Of course, because the family farm was in the middle of it all, it would be at the centre of everything that happened. South fork in Dallas wouldn't have a look in. The farm seemed to stay the same over the years with sheep and chickens being the farm's main income. We did rent out a lot of fields to local farmers to graze their dairy cattle. That was a regular income that helped out a lot as Mummy didn't want it to become a large business, because she always wanted to be able to run it herself. Most of that year, I was away overseas with the army and didn't get to go home at all, but that Christmas, I got well-earned extended leave because of all the time I spent in the field and I decided against all the warnings from the army to go home for Christmas and the New Year. I asked Mary if I could have Rosie for the holiday period and she said yes. She even made it over for Christmas day herself and then left

Rosie with me for the New Year. We had a great family holiday with the whole family together. Sammy was in good form and not drinking which made the atmosphere relaxing. Mummy looked so happy with all her boys and all her grandchildren around her and no doubt she was sad to see us all go. She had a sparkle in her eyes.

On Christmas morning, it was something special to see all the grandchildren visit the house and give out presents. We all gathered around the Christmas tree and watched Mummy give out the presents to everybody. Christmas music was playing in the background and the usual noise of children laughing and ripping the paper off presents with the look of excitement on their faces. The best one though was the look on Sammy's face when he opened his present from James and Jane. It was a new top-of-the-range video camera. If we thought he was bad before, we just had to wait ten minutes. He truly was like one of the children on Christmas morning. He loved it and set about becoming Steven Spielberg again. If I ever hear 'And action' again, I will scream. It truly was the perfect family Christmas. I looked over at my brothers one by one and every one of them looked so happy and content. Sammy Spielberg was running around with his new video camera doing his usual thing and enjoying every moment of it. To see him like that, you would never think the poor lad was an alcoholic and had a fight on his hands every day. A tear come to my eye out of happiness for him because he was a great lad who had been dealt a terrible hand as a young boy. At the usual time of ten o'clock, we all made our way to church. Twenty- five of us leaving together as one big happy family. As we walked into the church, we could hear the vicar saying, "There's a lot of them, isn't there?" We did giggle to ourselves but didn't take offence to it at all. I'm sure he was happy to see so many people at the service. When the church service was over, we stopped at Daddy's grave. We all gathered around his grave and reflected for a moment before we all laid a red rose. Twenty-five red roses for the man whom we have to thank for all we have in life. It was a lovely moment for us all not only for all the brothers but for Daddy's grandchildren. Daddy would be in tears of joy seeing his family that he created standing around him sending him so much love. As we left, we all looked around and shouted Merry Christmas to him. The sound of the trees made me think he was answering us. When we got back to the farm, Mummy noticed that Sammy was missing. "Did anyone see where Sammy went? I didn't see him walking up the road." I said I would go look for him. I knew where to look first. The graveyard. There is an old bench right behind Daddy's headstone that we all sit on when we visit Daddy. It is the place I would always go to when I need thinking time on my own. That's where he was sitting on his own talking to Daddy. I could hear him as I walked up the back lane. I sat down by his side and put my arm around him. He had tears in his eyes. "What's up, Sammy? Mummy sent me out to find you, lad."

"I'm in too deep, Stephen, and for the life of me I can't find a way out. It's going to kill me, but I can't give up now. It's gone too far to, and I can't go back now."

"What is it, Sammy? What are you talking about? Tell me what's wrong and I will help in any way I can."

Before I could get him to say anymore, he said, "Don't worry, Stephen, and forget about it. I'm just feeling emotional about the day. It's been so good, and I feel so happy. Come on let's get back home before there's no turkey left. That lot will skin it like a bloody piranha." We walked up the road laughing and joking as if the last half hour never happened. As we got to the door, Sammy turned to me and asked me to not tell anyone, especially Mummy, what we talked about.

"I will, Sammy, but I need to know what you meant by in too deep."

He grabbed me by the hand and said, "The drink, Stephen; I'm drinking way too much, and I can't stop but I will beat it someday, don't you worry." He gave me one of his great big hugs before he told me he loved me. I said the same back. We walked up the road having a laugh trying to pretend everything was okay, and as we got to the back door, he stopped me and asked me again to say nothing to Mummy. I promised him. "Look who I found wandering the road. Mr

Spielberg here was shooting his first scene for his new movie." That brought a roar of laughter to the house and calmed Mummy down. Sammy give me a wink and whispered, thank you. We always had our Christmas dinner at 3 p.m. after the Queen's speech and this time was no different. When we all gathered around the family table, John led us in prayer.

"Dear Lord,

Thank you for this table full of wonderful people.

Thank you for this table full of fabulous food.

Thank you for this table full of festive fellowship and

Thank you for looking after our dear loved ones in your presence. And dear Lord we thank you for looking after our Daddy in heaven. We love and miss him so very much. Thank you God, in Jesus name, Amen."

Mummy stood up and said, "Thank you, John. I feel blessed to have you all with me on this special day. Enjoy, everyone; Merry Christmas."

That evening, we all sat together telling and listening to stories. We laughed, cried and remembered all the people that were gone. The girls just listened to us telling stories of our youth and not believing what they were hearing. One story that I don't ever remember telling outside the family had everyone in stitches, even James. "I remember one time when I was about ten, James decided to build a go-cart."

All of a sudden, we could hear James at the back, "Aw, fuck me, no. I thought you shits forgot about that. Bollocks."

"Can I carry on please; it's my story."

"Right, fuck sake carry on but I will get you back, soldier boy."

"As I was saying, James decided to build a go-cart with an old pram Mummy had no use for. He started to make the frame with old timber and used the wheels and axels from the pram. Now you made a good job of it, James, and it worked brilliantly but there's one thing he forgot to do. He didn't hammer the ten-inch nails down properly. He hammered then upwards and bent them over. So, out he comes on his new machine and pushes it up to the top of the field at the back of the house. With his feet on the front tee bar and the steering rope, he asked us to push him off the top which we did. Now he had no brakes so when he got to the bottom he had set up a few hay bales to stop himself. Well, everything worked great. We run to the bottom and he was still on the go-cart but crying. 'What happened, it looked great?' He shouted at us to go away and the way he said it made us go away. It turns out that when he hit the bales, he slid up the go-cart and one of the bent nails impaled his ass to the go-cart. An hour later, he appeared holding his ass. He wouldn't let anyone help him, including Mummy." The place was in fits of laughter and even James was laughing.

"Don't you worry, boy, I'll get you back for that one." He took it well and laughed like everyone there. As some of the girls decided to go to bed, Mary came over to me when I was at the sink and said she would love me to spend the night with her. We had been separated for a few years but always got on great after the separation. She kissed me and said make sure you don't waken Rosie when you come in. We spent the night as a family but that's all it was. When most everyone had gone to bed apart from the six of us, John asked Sammy to get his video camera. He wanted us to do a video for Mummy wishing her all the love we had for her.

As we sat together, John said, "Stephen, we would love for you to speak because you're the most likely one not to be here next year." I slapped him on the back and thanked him. "We will all say something, but you take the lead." Sammy set up his new camera and for the first time we waited for him to say, "Action". We were having so much fun with this trying to get it right with Sammy learning on the job. Every time we thought we got it right, it was wrong. Fuckin' thing was taking forever. We eventually got it done and got a five-minute clip for Mummy to watch whenever she wanted to have a pick-me-up in life. I spoke from the heart, as did the other lads, and it showed the love we had for her and Daddy.

"No one will ever know the strength of our love for you. No one will ever know how much love we have for you.

You've gone through a lot of struggle and pain. But we promise you, we won't let all that go in vain. After all, you're the only one who knows what our heart beat sounds like. With all our hearts, we love you both." We all said our bit before Sammy finished it off.

"And we will never forget our promise to you, Mummy, never."

We all looked at him and knew exactly what he meant. Little did we know that it would be the last time we boys would be together and little did we know what was around the corner.

Chapter 9
Unwanted News

The year was now 2003 and, without doubt, at the beginning of the New Year, everything with the Richards family was great. The New Year brought new challenges for the shop and garage as it tried to keep up with the changing technologies in their line of business. The development of machinery was changing at an alarming rate and Daddy's shop was most definitely an old school business. The shop moved with the times but tried to hold on to the old ways because that's what most of the local farmers did. The tractors got bigger and bigger and the machinery that the farmers used had to develop in the same way. The good thing about the shop and garage was that they hired people that moved with the times. Young people that knew what they were doing with the development of farm machinery and with the evolution of the business. They were few and far between but because Daddy's business also had old school ways about it as well it appealed to them, so even though it was difficult for them they moved with the times and became a business for old and new farmers. That pleased Uncle Alan because he most definitely was of the old school fraternity. Sammy was still working at the garage but was not fulltime. He would never think about going to the garage or shop with drink in him and decided to stay away. Billy filled that gap easily, so the business kept going well. Mummy was still a silent owner at the beginning of 2003 but decided to hand over all her shares and interest in the business to James and Billy, with a stipulation that Sammy was always going to have a share in the business no matter how he was doing. Mummy had all she needed with the farm and her family around her. We lost a family member at the beginning of February but it's one we didn't have much sympathy with. Granny D was found close to death one Sunday morning. She was found by Aunty Ruth and Uncle Paddy who were calling to pick her up for chapel. Mummy did get the chance to visit Granny D the day before she died. Aunty Mary called at the house to tell Mummy she was close to death and would she call and see her before she passed away. She did and right away. When she got to the house, some of her brothers and sisters made themselves scarce so as not to have to speak to her. That was the siblings that took Granny D's side in the past. She was told that she had no voice but could see and hear okay. As Mummy entered the room, she could see that her mum was indeed on her death bed. She leaned into her and spoke to her from the heart. "I want to let you know that I forgive you, but I don't imagine that God will. Your forgiveness 'if you have any' will not save you, mother dear." She kissed her on the forehead and left the room not looking back. The priest thanked Mummy for her doing what God would have asked of her. "Did you ask my mother the same question, Father?" There was no response from him. Mummy left that house with her head held high and the eyes of her siblings cutting her to pieces. That was the depth of division within their family circle. I know what was said because Mummy made no secret of it and told the lads. There was no surprise to us that Mummy was not that upset but we all knew, however, that she would be upset in her own way, but it you think of what Granny D put her through over the years, you will understand her feelings. Mummy didn't go to the wake but chose to go to the funeral. She asked James, Sammy, Billy, John and Boyd if they would support her at the funeral. They all said yes apart from Billy. Billy had too much of a background with loyalists linked to the UVF. That was a step too far for him but Mummy totally agreed with him declining and most likely secretly wanted that. On the day of the funeral, Mummy knew what to expect and was ready to silence everyone who would be intent on making her uncomfortable. As they arrived at the house, they were all welcomed at the doorstep by Uncle Paddy who was with the local priest—the same priest who stood up for Mummy in the past. He thanked her for her forgiveness and doing the right thing in the eyes of the lord. There were no sweets from Paddy this time because men now stood where children did before. There was only a handshake. As the coffin left the house, the sons and sons-in-law took the first lift of the coffin. As they got out of sight of her house, the undertaker asked for the fourth group of lifters to come forward. No one knew it was four of Mummy's sons until they stepped forward and took the lift. That did not go down well with a lot of people there, especially Mummy's brothers and sisters that did not side with her. The shock on faces was plain to see and the lads didn't give a shit. They all had a grin of satisfaction on their faces compared to the shock on everyone else's. Mummy walked with Aunty Mary and Joyce a few rows back. She had the last laugh. Before the funeral started, Mummy spoke with the undertaker who was arranging the different lifts to make sure her sons took their turn. That was the talk of the town for quite some time after.

When the month of March started, Mummy had an appointment at the local surgery because she had a pain in her side. Nothing to worry about because Mummy said it was pain from when she fell over chasing the chickens around the farm. It wasn't the first time she or many of us fell over chasing chickens around the farmyard but this time there was something else. Two weeks after the appointment, she had a visit by the same doctor she'd seen in the surgery. He checked her over and suggested she make an appointment to get a scan. She said not to brother as it was only a bang and that it would clear up in a few weeks. He warned against her doing nothing and not getting a scan, but as usual, Mummy knew best. She told him if it wasn't better in a few weeks, she would make an appointment to see him again. It was left like that but knowing the doctor as we do, he would be on her case until she did. She kept it quiet and never told any of us, but by the end of March, the pain was still there. Jane called at the farmhouse one day, and she was still in bed not being able to get out because of the pain. She immediately called the doctor, and it was the same doctor who suggested she had a scan the first time round. When he arrived the first thing he said to her was I thought you told me you would call me if it hadn't cleared up, Rose. Jane turned to him and asked him what he meant. She was so angry when he told her Mummy's decision at the beginning of March. Within the hour, Jane had Mummy at the hospital for an emergency scan. She spent the night in hospital because the pain was so bad and because the scan could throw up something bad that needed immediate attention. Two days later, Mummy got to go home but she was still waiting for the results of the scan. She had very strong pain killers to take which meant she was bedridden for a while. The doctor called at the house a week later to see Mummy and to give her the results. He made sure that Jane or someone else was with her so that Mummy didn't pull the same stunt again. He checked her over first and seemed happy that the pain was subsiding quite a bit. The next thing he said was the beginning of a bad time for us. "Listen, Rose, something has showed up in the scan that needs looking at. There's a shadow on your lungs that we need to do a biopsy on; it's only a small procedure but we need to get it done as soon as possible." Mummy looked so shocked at the news, but Jane was so strong and supportive of her.

"Don't worry, Rose, it's most likely only a cyst. So, when will that be, Doctor?" He had already booked the surgery for the next day. The next evening, with the lot of us at the hospital, Mummy had her small operation. It was just to take a small sample of lung tissue for analysis. She was in one day and out the next. It was just a matter of time now. I wasn't told until it was diagnosed because I was in Iraq on active duty. When I did get word about the situation, I wanted to go back home there and then but when I spoke to Mummy she said it was all cleared up and nothing to worry about, but knowing what Mummy's like, I called James to find out the real story. He firstly told me that it was silly to come home as there was nothing to do but wait so that's what I did. It didn't stop me from worrying, though. I also needed to concentrate

100% on my own situation as I was in a war zone. I didn't need the worry of not knowing what was going on back home with Mummy. Around two weeks later, Mummy got the news and it was not good. She had lung cancer. It was a hammer blow for us all. I, though, wasn't told for two weeks because I could not be contacted as I was in charge of an ongoing operation in the field. The major informed me when got back from the operation and immediately got me some leave to go back home. I was home within the week. Mummy had already had a small operation to remove a lump and was well on her way to recover from it; however, the realisation that that was only the beginning of her treatment made her feel down. With the whole family around her, she was again upbeat about her treatment and recovery. The doctors informed us that everything was going to plan and that Mummy's first treatment of chemotherapy would begin as soon as she was well enough after her operation. "What does she have, Doctor, and how bad is it?"

"Your mum has what's referred to as small-cell lung cancer and it's usually treated with chemotherapy, sometimes in combination with radiotherapy depending on the severity and how it reacts to the treatment, but we feel positive that we got all the cancerous cell and bad tissue out during the operation." We all felt as positive as we could, but you always think the worst when cancer is involved. She was home now and we all surrounded her with love and made sure she had everything she needed. I only had five days leave in total, with only one day left, so I was glad I had the full story and could rely on the whole family helping out; well, so I thought. I'd been home for four days now and still hadn't seen or heard from Sammy. You would think with the situation he would be around Mummy all day, being a right pain in the arse. When I was told where he was, I was so pissed off with him. Sammy was on a bender and had been since Mummy was diagnosed. He just couldn't take the news, which I can understand, and turned to the drink to blank it all out. The last day of my leave I went looking for him and I found him sleeping in the large barn up in the hay loft with a bottle of vodka by his side. I took the bottle off him and lobbed it down at the old cement mixer below. That got his attention right away, as he hadn't yet had his morning drink. He looked at me like a rabbit caught in light. "What the fuck are you doing, Sammy? Mummy is in there with her whole world collapsing around her and you're out here fucking drunk. For days now, I've been home and not caught sight of you once. Are you fucking serious, lad? Get yourself down that ladder, try to sober up, get cleaned up and get into that house and show Mummy you're okay. She has enough on her plate without fucking worrying about you as well. Jesus Christ, Sammy, man up. Mummy needs your support." I leaned over him and looked him in the eye. "This time tomorrow, I will be half way round the world preparing to fight some other fucker's battle. I will be in the field fighting a bunch of mad fuckin rag head cunts intent on cutting my goddamn head off and the last goddamn thing I need is to not only worry about Mummy but you as well. Fuck that shit, boy. I have never raised my voice to you before, Sammy, and I've always had your back, but this time it's different. This time it's Mummy. She needs us all to be there for her but listen lad, as well you know I'm not going to be here for her, so I need you to be twice as strong for her. Please Sammy, for my sake and Mummy's." He never looked at me once he just got down the ladder and just stared at the ground. I held out my hand waiting for him to shake it. He was hesitant at first but eventually did. "Promise me, Sammy. I need to hear you say it, lad, say it."

"I promise, Stephen. God help me, I promise. I have my reasons for drinking, Stephen, none of which are good; put it this way, I need to reach up to touch the bottom some days. That's how low I can be at times. At the moment Stephen it feels like my only true friend is my shadow. It goes everywhere with me, never talks down to me and never leaves my side." I put my arms around him and squeezed him tightly.

"You couldn't be further from the truth, Sammy. You are loved so much by us all, but if you don't sort this out Sammy, you will know it. Without doubt, you will know it."

As I walked out the barn I met Billy on his way in. "Where is that fuckin' waste of space. Enough is enough. I'm not letting him put Mummy through any more of this shit." I tried to stop him, but that lad is as strong as a raging bull. He pushed me aside and went for Sammy and before I could stop him he had him up against the wall screaming blue hell at him. I grabbed Billy by the neck to get him off but it was like a monkey grabbing an elephant. The three of us lost balance and hit the floor before I got Billy to let go of Sammy. I shouted for Sammy to go into the house which he did. I held onto Billy as long as I could, waiting for Sammy to get away. "Billy stop please, you're making matters worse here." We got up and before I knew it he fired a right hook at my head and down I went. Fuck me; it was like a hammer blow and I was seeing three of him.

"If you ever put your hands on me again, I will take your head off, understand?"

My reply was direct. "Next time you swing at me make sure I stay down because if I get up I will snap your fuckin leg in two Billy." As I said before, he was a bull of a man with no fear and a man I could never handle but I had to let him know with my training I knew what I was doing. He stormed off leaving me to get my marbles back, which took ten minutes at least. I walked into the house as if nothing happened, packed my gear to go before I spoke to Mummy. She was as usual cleaning the kitchen and being the boss in her own home. "Mummy, I need to get going here. Will you be okay?"

"Don't you worry about me, Stephen; I have all I need and who I need around me but please be careful wherever you go. I worry so much, and I couldn't cope with losing another one."

"I will, Mummy. I will. It's a lot safer where I'm going and I'm on the back line giving orders now." I said goodbye to each and every one there, knowing that the next time we met it could be for Mummy's end. Both Sammy and Billy said goodbye to me and both wished me well and to be safe even after what just occurred; they are my brothers and our bond is strong. As I made my way back to Belfast to catch my first flight back to camp I could not get out of my mind what I had left behind. Was I ever to see Mummy's face again? Would Sammy come through for us and clean up his act or would I ever see his face again? The worry of battle and looking after my own ass would take over my thoughts and help me through this. Before I left England, I went to see Mary and Rosie. I only had twenty-four hours at base before my plane left for Iraq. I told her what had happened and about Mummy which broke her heart. I asked her to be my ears and eyes and to tell me the truth even if it was bad and I was in the field. I could rely on Mary for her honesty knowing she would do what needed to be done on my behalf. I cried the night through with Mary by my side listening to me. It's not the first time she was my rock. Next morning, Mary said to me, "Make sure you come back to us, Stephen. You're always in our prayers, darling." I said my goodbyes to them both before I made my way back to base to catch the plane to Iraq. What the rest of the year had in store for us who knows, but what doesn't kill us will only make us stronger. I just hope that's true.

Chapter 10
Back with Daddy

Sitting in a stinking dusty hole in the middle of Iraq with nothing but the smell of shit to keep us company, I started to question myself on why the fuck I was fighting some other fucker's war. I only had questions and not one answer to any of them. I looked around at my platoon sitting in the same shit-ridden hole wondering if they were thinking the same thing. My corporal, who's called Smithy, looked over at me waiting for my orders, his lips moving, but there was no sound. I could see some of them crawling in a ball each time the place shook and some just getting on with it. Some of the lads were downing as much water as they could, and others were reloading their weapons. Me? My mind and thoughts were back in the Cross wondering how Mummy was and if Sammy was even alive. I found myself in a place I had been many times before looking for tranquillity, peace and answers but the answers just weren't there this time—our church graveyard in the Cross where Daddy was buried. This time I could only see smoked filled visions of what looked like mounds of dirt beside Daddy's grave. My vision got less and less as the smoke raised over me leaving me blinded with a yellow mist and not being able to see my hand before me. My place of peace had no peace to offer me this time. As I waited for it to clear, it was like waiting for someone to turn up the volume as well. As it cleared I could see Smithy approaching me and yelling in my face but still there was no sound, then the place shook with a tremendous velocity and filled the hole again with sandy dust. That took me out of the stupor I was in and just as quickly as it happened I was back in reality again.

The sound was back on and my visions were back in the reality of the situation. I was in a war zone and under attack. "Waiting for your orders, sir. We need to move and move now. They're on both sides of us, Lieutenant." I was back in control of myself and gave the orders.

"Smithy, get some smoke out there and tell the lads to go on my command. We will make for the compound next to the vehicles at twelve o'clock. Get two lads to give covering fire to the left and two to the right, we go in one minute. Okay, Smithy, smoke." With the smoke now laid down and giving us cover, I gave the command for the covering fire. Five seconds later, I shouted, "On me." We belted out of the hole and made our way to the compound. "Okay, Smithy, prepare for covering fire again. Ready lads, on my command make your way to us, covering fire." The noise was deafening as the four lads that give us covering fire retreated to our position. "Everyone okay, lads? Smithy?"

"Yes, sir, all good."

"Right then, let's make our way back to the OP (Observation post). Smithy, make sure everyone is with us." We got there in one piece and with no injuries. When we got back to base, the major wanted a debrief update on what happened and what went wrong. "It's simple, sir. The intel was wrong, the timing was wrong and the idea that we could just wander into that area unchecked was madness. They probably knew we were coming before we left the bloody barracks, sir. It smelt wrong from the beginning and that's not because the first explosion went off in their fucking shit hole which incidentally we had to jump into. We walked into an ambush with the enemy on both sides, waiting for us to appear. How the fuck no one was killed is beyond me. They most likely were blinded with the fucking smell of their shit hole blowing up. We dived for cover in a large hole just south of a compound and returned fire. It took us, or should I say me, a few minutes to get my bearings and assess the situation, but Corporal Smithy was on the ball right away. He got smoke out there, had covering fire ready to be laid down before getting me up to speed. We retreated to the compound and from there back to the OP. No casualties or injuries to report, sir."

"Are you telling me they blew up their own latrine hole?"

"Yes, sir, they did, which we jumped into for cover."

"Lovely. Okay, get yourselves washed up and we can have a full debrief later on. I don't think I can put up with that smell for much longer."

"Thank you, sir; as always, it was a pleasure." As Smithy and I left, he whispered, smug cunt to me and yes he was but to his credit he had helped out each and every one of us when we needed it, smug cunt or not. The 2003 invasion of Iraq lasted from 20 March to 1 May 2003 and signalled the start of the Iraq War, which was dubbed Operation Iraqi Freedom, but the fight went on for another eight long years The Iraq War was a protracted conflict that began in 2003 with the invasion of Iraq by a US-led coalition. It initially overthrew Saddam Hussein, but the conflict continued for much of the next decade as an insurgency emerged to oppose the occupying forces after the invasion of Iraq. It was a battle that took a lot of lives and still today has no sign of ending. I was beginning to spend more time there than I was everywhere else combined, but my mind and heart was back home. I was fighting someone else's battles and Mummy was fighting hers. That's where my mind and heart was. It was coming to the end of 2003 and no sight of my deployment ending, but yet another goddamn unwanted phone call from back home at the beginning of December would take me back home and this time with news I didn't want to hear. This time I got the news from the unit's chaplain that I have to place a call to my brother James as soon as I could. I just knew it was going to be bad and couldn't for the life of me see a scenario where it could be good. After the chaplain left, I gathered my thoughts about what had happened back home and how I was going to deal with it. It had to be Mummy. When I left, she was still getting chemo for her cancer but then I thought, everything was looking good, the operation was a success, the treatment was working, Mummy was in good form, so what the hell could have gone wrong. I was going through every bad thought possible but always ended up with Mummy. I had no choice; I had to make the call and deal with it. The time I spent waiting for that call to connect felt like an eternity to me and my stomach was churning. Here was me, just back from the battlefield where I no doubt took the lives of the enemy shitting myself about what news I was about to hear and then a voice spoke. "Hello?"

"Hello James, it's Stephen."

"Stephen, how you doing lad?"

"I'm okay, James, but somehow I think the next thing out of your mouth is going to make me not okay." He paused before his voice started to break up. "Fuck it, James, tell me, is it Mummy?"

The next three words were such a relief to me and I felt like the heavy load was just lifted off me. "No, it's not. It's Sammy; there's no easy way to say this Stephen, we found him dead this morning."

"Sweet Jesus," I shouted. I went cold from within, not knowing what to say or do. The silence was deafening to me.

"Are you okay, Stephen?" James said as he cried. I just could not speak or think. "Listen, if you can get yourself home to us, we will wait for you before we do anything." I tried to speak but it just came out like a gargled whisper. "Just get home, Stephen. We will explain everything when you get here. Mummy's asking for you."

All I could say was, "Okay." That was it. I didn't ask about Mummy even after thinking the worst before the call. I just said okay. The chaplain was outside the call booth with the major waiting for me, knowing the news already. He took me into his room and did their best to comfort me, but I was still dumbfounded and silent. "Let's get you home, Lieutenant," said the major who again, even though we called him a smug cunt, was there for me.

"Thanks, sir." Those were the only words I could speak. The chaplain sat beside me and started to pray for me and my family and his ending words got me to face up to the situation. The words 'we pray for your poor mother' immediately got my attention. What was she going through back there? I got up right away and said, "I need to go; I need to get home now." I rushed out, went straight to my digs and packed as little as I needed. I met Smithy on my way out and didn't even stop to tell the news but by the look on his face, he knew. He shouted at me as I got into the jeep.

"Godspeed, sir." He knew. I looked back without acknowledging him as we drove off and he saluted me. At least I had the wits about me to salute him back, but I think that was a built-in habit. The whole journey back was a complete blank to me. I don't remember a moment of it. A salute from Smithy to getting off the helicopter in Belfast— that's my only memory of the journey. I stepped off the helicopter in Belfast still in my battle gear, it went that fast. The snow was thick on the ground and the sharp breeze would cut you in two. I was told to go and change before my onward journey, which I did. I didn't realise I was in my battle gear until I was told. As I got to the gates of the barracks, I could see James and Boyd inside the compound waiting for me. This was not going to be good. I walked up to them both before we all embraced. We cried our hearts out for Sammy. He didn't deserve to die so young and after the start in life he had as well. "Come on, let's get home. Mummy's waiting for you." It took me twenty-four hours to get to Belfast and the next hour and a half would be the longest with the long and winding roads we had to take. I sat in the back with James and he explained everything to me. Boyd was up front with James's lad Bill.

"What happened to him, James?"

"He was found dead at the bottom of the hedge next to the church. He had been there all night. It looks like he fell in to the hedge full drunk, fell asleep and never woke up; in short, he froze to death. The poor fucker just fell asleep, God love him." I was in shock and stunned at what happened to him.

"How long was he there before he was found?" I asked.

"According to the police report, he left the pub before midnight and never made it home, so if you say it should have taken him at most ten minutes to get to the church which is in the other direction from his home. He was most likely in that bloody hedge from midnight. He was found at 9 a.m. next morning." The thought crossed my mind trying to understand it.

I asked James, "Was he hit by a car or beat up and thrown in the hedge?"

"There are no signs of foul play, Stephen, and we can tell that he was up at Daddy's grave just before because of the tracks in the snow. Just his tracks up and his tracks down. Also, where he was found the grass verge by the road was still covered in snow so the police said it was very unlikely foul play was involved. I'm just glad Mummy didn't go to the grave as usual to see Daddy because she could have been the one to find him."

"And how's Mummy doing?" I asked.

"As you can imagine, lad, she's in a mess. The doctor has given her something to keep her calm but that won't last for long. All she keeps saying is that William will look after him now. He'll be okay from now on, so he will. We have to let her keep thinking that because that's her only saving grace at the moment. To be honest, we did see something like this coming, Stephen. This last while he was on such a bender. And I mean a bender. He's been drunk for the last three months, and he's took a lot of beatings this last few months as well, going places where he shouldn't fuckin' be and all he would keep saying is I'm close, just leave me be and you will see."

"What the fuck does that mean? Maybe he knew his end was near and was prepared for it." Both James and Boyd agreed but it still sounded strange to me. All I kept saying to myself was, "The poor bastard. He did not deserve that." Boyd was quiet in the front and not saying much which was understandable. He just kept looking to the road ahead. "How are you doing, Boyd? You're very quiet, lad." He looked at me in the inside mirror and just shook his head no. I grabbed him by the shoulder and let him know I felt his pain. We were all the same when it came to the pain from losing a loved one.

"Not long now," Boyd said to young Bill in the front seat.

"Bugger. Sorry, Bill, I completely forgot you were there. You're so small in that seat I couldn't see you. How are you doing, young man?" I asked.

"I'm all right, Uncle Stephen. Just a bit cold," he said.

"Turn on the heat for the lad, Boyd. We can't have you freezing to death on us Bill. Fuck," I'd just realize realised what I just said. "Sorry, lads. Bad choice of words there." James slapped me on the leg and just told me not to worry. Easy done he said. Young Bill never got what I said, thank God. As we got closer to home, I asked if Sammy's body was home yet and was told he would be on his way tonight from the morgue.

"We will be leaving for the morgue round about five, Stephen. We have everything planned and sorted, even your suit. He will be laid to rest tomorrow beside Daddy."

Daddy? I said to myself. "He's not going to be alone anymore."

"Nearly there," Boyd said, looking at young Bill in the front seat. "You can snuggle up in front of the open fire and that will warm you up, cub." That's one thing I always missed after I left home. There was nothing like a big warm turf fire in the winter time. Hearing Boyd say that took me back to when we were young lads and we all had to go out on the Bog to help cut the turf with Daddy and our uncles. It was always a family thing. We would get together and cut the Turf, grow the spuds and cut the hay. If I remember right, Daddy called it making the Haycocks. Still sounds just as wrong as it did back then. It was always the whole family. I remember when we were in the bog cutting turf asking uncle James when we would be getting paid for the work we had done and he said, "See when you get cold in the winter time and you crawl up in front of the fire to get warm, that's your pay, cub." It all made sense when I was cold.

As we drove through the small windy roads towards home, I started to think back our youth and had visions of us playing as children, playing in the fields, running up and down the lanes, the six of us kicking a ball or racing bicycles up and down. What I would give for those times again. As we turned for the last set of bends I could see someone standing at the end of the lane next to the last corner. Of course, it was still a vision, but it was a vision of Sammy. It was Sammy as a boy and he was looking at me with a smile on his face as we passed by. The tears started to flow down my face as the memories and home became closer and closer. "Stephen, Stephen, we're home lad." I was in a world of my own when James shook me and never noticed we had stopped in the yard at the back of the house. I was home and for the first time I didn't want to be. Getting out of the car and walking up to the back door I knew everything was about to get real because up to now it was like a bad dream. I was last to enter the house and the first person I saw was Mummy. She was sitting at the top of the kitchen on a stool with people around her. I was shocked and could not believe what I was seeing. She was so small and looked like she had aged twenty years since I'd last seen her. The treatment for her cancer had taken its toll on her and the news of Sammy dragged her down even more. I so wanted to stop and go back outside and cry because of the look of sadness and pain on her face but I couldn't. She spotted me as if she was waiting for me to get home. She held out her arms and cried my name. It was a cry that I will never forget and a cry that will break my heart whenever I think of it. As I got to her, my emotions took over and I was like a little kid running to the arms of my Mummy again. As I embraced her, I could feel her small brittle body and the pain she had inside. I was on my knees with my head on her left shoulder and a feeling came over me that instantly made sense. I could feel a warm presence on her left shoulder that instantly made me feel at ease. If someone was to explain to me that they had just felt what I had I would laugh at them. I felt the presence of Sammy with Mummy and he was like her guardian angel now, repaying her for all the years she looked out for him. Now the vision of Sammy on the lane made pure sense. He would stay with Mummy to help her through. From that moment I believed it and when I explained to Mummy what I'd seen and felt she was to become so strong and ready to face the next few days. I looked up at the gathering family waiting to greet me and every single person was in tears. They had heard me and, no doubt, believed in what I'd said. As I stood up, Mummy stood up with me and just dropped into my arms. The family gathered in and as one we cried for Sammy. The silence of the kitchen was broken and though it was broken with crying, sadness, tears, it was a family as one in tears. It was time to gather around each other and use the inner strength we had as a broken family.

One by one I embraced my brothers and I was glad I had them to lean on as I'm sure they were of me. Then I looked into the hallway only to see Mary standing there with a tray of biscuits talking to well-wishers. She came running to me, tray and all, and wrapped her arms around me. It was so wonderful to have her there and give Mummy and me the support we needed. She looked so upset and just wanted to hold me. "Thank you, Mary. This is so sweet of you honey, but can I have a cup of tea with my biscuits?" She just smiled a little and gave me the sweetest kiss before helping me remove the broken biscuits from my hair. I started to thank people in the house and to say the house was jammed full would be an understatement.

I only got as far as the kitchen door when John shouted, "Stephen, you need to get ready because we need to get to the morgue for Sammy. Your suit is in the back room with ours." Mary put her tray down and took me by the hand upstairs, past everyone who wanted to speak to me. We just didn't have the time. As we got to the top of the stairs at the back room, I stopped. "What's wrong, Stephen?" I started to shake with fear. "What's wrong, Stephen? You're shaking, darling." She grabbed me and put her arms around me tightly. "It's not the first time I've walked into this room empty. It's not the first time it's been emptied for a dead person. Daddy was waked in this room and I remember watching as my uncles emptied the room for Daddy. Now my brothers are doing the same thing, only now it's for one of us." Billy came out the door and put his arm around me and led me inside. He closed the door and we all got dressed.

As we finished getting ready, Billy stepped forward, "Let's go and get Sammy and bring him home, boys." We gathered as one before leaving for the Morgue. "Mummy, we're off to get Sammy and bring him home." She looked at us as if to say don't be long and be careful just like she always did.

"We will look after her, boys, don't you worry," said Jane. The three girls would treat Mummy as their own mums.

As we got to the morgue, Billy turned to us in the back seat and told us, "Hold your nerve lads and be proud of Sammy. Let no fucker whisper rumours behind our backs or talk shit to our faces. That boy deserves the best and we will give it to him. Heads up for Sammy."

"This was not going to be easy," I said to John. "Can I have some of your faith, John? I don't think I can do this."

He grabbed me by the arm and said, "Sammy's with us Stephen, didn't you say so yourself? Just believe he's walking amongst us and we'll get through." They were very helping words. It was just us five boys to see Sammy at first as we wanted to be alone with him and as we entered, there he was, just as if he was sleeping. In my head, I was saying, "Wake up, Sammy," and hoping he would do so but I knew he wouldn't. One by one we went forward and kissed him on the forehead and said our goodbyes to him. We all held our nerve and kept our heads high as Billy said. The gathering mourners started to came in and pay their respects and it went on and on until we had to make a move as the undertaker said time had come and gone to get underway. We carried Sammy into the hearse and made our way home with him. The crowds of people were unreal as we left the mortuary and according to the police the road to the Cross was blocked for an hour to let the mourners' cars through. Reaching the house, it went through our minds that this would be Sammy's last home coming and indeed James said that as we entered the gates. Thousands of people lined the lane and surrounded the house as we drove in and all the joining roads and lanes were full. We were so proud of the thought that Sammy had touched so many people in his short and troubled life.

"Right, here we go lads, home again." Billy took the lead as we took the coffin up the stairs and into the back room and as like Daddy, the minister blessed the coffin as we sat him down. We stood back as the undertaker lifted the lid to let us make sure everything was okay, and as we did, Jane and Grace came into the room with Mummy.

"Where's Sammy, where is he, awk there you are, my wee pet. My wee Sammy." This was the hardest thing to take, not being able to help Mummy with her pain. She turned and looked at us. "Thank you, my boys. Look after him now he's home, won't you?"

"Don't worry, Mummy; we will," said Boyd. James asked that at least one of us was to stay in the room with Sammy to greet people.

"I'll stay first lads. I want to spend some time with him just to catch up with him."

"Good man, Stephen. Come on lads, let's give Stephen a few minutes before people start coming in." I had so much that I wanted to say but I just cried the whole time. It was a release of emotions that took over me and I had no control. Here was a man who faced the enemy under fire and took the lives of men in battle without a second thought. Before I knew it, the door opened and mourners started filling the room. It was non-stop and before I knew it, two hours had passed. Mary came in and said, "Come on, Stephen; time for a cup of tea." That sounded so good because it would be the first cup of tea since I left the airport for Belfast.

"Sweet Jesus, where have they all come from?" The house, back yard, front yard, driveway and roads were full of cars and people. I have never seen the likes of it. I sat at the table with some of our relations and enjoyed my first cup of tea. "Mary, can I have them biscuits now?" She turned to me and gave me a bugger off grin, which lifted my mood.

I got a tray of everything I wanted sat in front of me and a voice said, "I'm going to have to stop doing this for you, Stephen." I looked up and it was Aunty Sally. My favourite Aunty of them all. I still have fond memories staying with her family when I was a little boy. We hugged and talked for so long catching up on old times as it's been years since I'd last seen her. Ten cups of tea later, it was time to close the house down. It was 12.30 a.m. and we had a long day tomorrow. During the night, because off all the bloody tea I had, I got up to go to the loo only to find the past coming back to me again. As I walked past the back room where Sammy was, I heard a voice from behind the closed door. It was Mummy who was in with Sammy and she was crying her heart out, but not only that, she was talking to him as if he was still alive. Then I did something that was in my mind. I just sat down outside the door and quietly listened to her crying. I had done this before many times and it just felt normal. Before long, John, who was staying in the house as well, heard Mummy and joined me sitting outside the door. We just sat there listening and doing or saying nothing. Mary came out to see where I was and just couldn't believe we were doing what I always talked to her about. "Come on, Stephen; we need to get to bed. Tomorrow is only hours away." We knocked on the door to get Mummy and she was asleep in the chair beside Sammy. We took her to bed with Mary's help, knowing tomorrow was a day that she would need all her strength for.

At 9 a.m. the house was getting ready for yet another funeral. We all had to get ready early because the funeral was to begin at midday. We let Mummy sleep as long as possible because of the day ahead of her and it was going to be a long day. At 10.30 a.m. both Mary and Jane helped Mummy get ready and the house was already full of family and friends waiting to say goodbye to Sammy. All us boys were already out and about, preparing to get underway and making sure that Sammy's last day was going to go as well as possible. At 11.30 a.m. it was time to say our goodbyes to Sammy. We joined Mummy in the back room along with the vicar to say the last prayer and close the coffin up. As we did, Mummy, who was very calm leaned into the coffin and kissed him goodbye. Her last words to him were, "Thank you for making my life worth living my wee miracle man and for keeping your promise to your daddy. Tell him I love him, and I will see him soon." We all said goodbye and watched as the undertakers closed the lid and Sammy's face would be gone forever. The long road ahead was full of people wishing to say goodbye as we carried Sammy to be with Daddy and as we did it brought back all those memories of Daddy's funeral but we had to be strong and pull through for Mummy's sake. The church was full, and the grounds were just as bad with people standing on the snow-covered grass. We walked into the church with Sammy's favourite song, 'It's a Kind of Magic' by Queen playing over the speakers which he would listen to all the time. It made us all smile thinking of Sammy dancing and singing along to it every time he put it on and the joy he brought to us all. Even Mummy had a little smile on her face which would only help her to no end. Like Daddy's funeral, it was a blur to me as I kept thinking of all the fun we had as children and still imagining Sammy watching over Mummy. As we sang the last song, 'Abide With Me', it hit me hard but only because of all the military funerals I'd been to of troops killed in battle. Mary grabbed me because she could see that I was struggling with it all and I bloody needed it as well. I looked to Mummy and she had her right hand on her left shoulder drawing the strength from her guardian angel. We all stood up and lifted Sammy aloft. Uncle Sam helped to make six carriers to carry him out to join Daddy. As we got to the edge of the grave and put Sammy down, I could see the little wooden box that now had Daddy's remains in it. We all knelt down and touched the lid which had Daddy's nameplate on it. Mummy kissed her fingers before touching the nameplate.

"Hello, my sweet darling. It's your turn to look after Sammy. See you soon, my love." With all the prayers done, we lowered Sammy into the ground with tears blinding us and saying farewell for the last time. James and Billy lowered Daddy in alongside Sammy before the last prayer. "You gave him life, Lord, now receive him in your peace and give him, through Jesus Christ, a joyful resurrection." We all dropped two roses onto the coffin, one for Daddy and one for Sammy. The terrorist attack that happened nearly twenty-five years ago had claimed its second victim. Sammy was just another name on the list of dead because of the troubles in Ulster. As we made our way home, Mummy, who was sitting in the front seat staring out the side window, spoke to the five of us, not taking her eyes from the passing view. "He did his best. Part of Sammy died that day in the car with William, but he never gave up. He just never gave up, bless him."

Chapter 11
Hammer Blow

The day after Sammy's funeral, the five of us had a chat about the last four days and what it had done to Mummy's health. We were all worried about how the treatment was going and if she had given up on life. That seemed to be the thought of us all after seeing how she was on the day of the funeral and on what John and I heard her saying to Sammy in his coffin the night before his funeral. She just kept saying to Sammy, "We will be together again soon, my brave wee darling". The outcome of the chat was that we needed to be around her as much as possible for the next year or so or until she got the all clear. After chatting to the lads and then to Mary, I decided that it was now time for Mummy to come first. Mary agreed with me and even though this didn't have anything to do with our on/off relationship, it would only help if indeed we did get back together. I decided to ask for a posting back to the UK and see out my last years in the army until I could get my full pension. That was only 2 years away. That night, which was my last night before leaving for the UK, I told all my brothers and Mummy my decision. Mummy was over the moon knowing I would be out of harm's way and be able to lead a normal life at last. My whole adult life was in the army and I would need time to adjust. "Mary, does this mean you and Stephen will get back together for good?" Mummy asked. "I hope so, Rose, I really do because I love Stephen with all my heart and it's only the army life that pulled us apart and if that's not there anymore, I don't see why not." They both hugged, leaving me overwhelmed at the thought of getting my family back together. Again, as I have done too many times before, I said goodbye. I left with Mummy in high spirits knowing she was getting her son back for good. I turned to the lads and asked them to let me know how Mummy was doing and if I was needed home. I did have some leave coming up soon so that would be something for Mummy to look forward to. Billy and Boyd left Mary and me at the airport for the flight home. "You look after yourselves and Billy, please be careful, lad." He hugged me hard.

"Don't worry, Stephen; I know what I'm doing."

"Time to go," said Mary. When we got back, I decided to speak to General Reed and tell him my decision. He was a bit surprised but totally understood my decision. "I will be sad to see you go, Sergeant, but I understand your situation. Family is very important, and it should always take precedence over everything else, but that's my view and not the army's, saying that, you need to go back and finish off your tour first Sergeant; you still have a job to do over there. I think I'm right in saying you have three months left."

"Yes, sir."

"Okay, then I will look to get you back to the UK when your tour's over. We can decide on what role we will have for then, for your remaining time. You ship out 1300 hours tomorrow." I was relieved that he was so understanding of my situation, but I would rather have not gone back to Iraq. That shit hole is the last place I wanted to be.

"Thank you, sir." I saluted and made my way out.

"Sergeant?"

"Yes, sir."

"I hope everything works out for the best for you and your family. Families are important." That meant a lot.

"Thank you, Major."

I spent the last night with Mary and Rosie before I left. "Can we do it Mary, can we be a family again after this is all done?" She looked at me as I sat there with Rosie in my arms.

"That is my dream, Stephen. You're a good man and someone who I want in our lives until we are old and grey." A family is important, just as the major said.

It only seemed like yesterday that I was on a chinook leaving the camp in Iraq to go back for Sammy's funeral and now here I was on the same bloody chinook going back to camp in Iraq. Time was that fast. I was back in this shit-infested, smelly flea hole, fighting a war I just didn't want to fight. The first face I saw was Smithy waiting for me as we landed. "Glad to have you back, sir. The place has gone to shit without you." I laughed because he was referring to the shitty bomb hole we got stuck in before I got called away.

"Well, fuck you too, Smithy," I said with a smile.

"Come on, sir, let's get you up to scratch with what's been going on here." Before he got the chance, I told him what I had set in motion.

"Fuck me, sir; are you sure you want to do that? Soldiering has been your life and you know that. Don't get me wrong; I admire your decision but fuck me, sir, with the greatest respect to your family that's not something you can decide in six days." I understood where Smithy was coming from, but my mind was made up.

"Sorry, Smithy, my decision is final, and the paperwork is underway. I have recommended you to take over the squad when I leave. You're the only man that the lads trust and know. I'm not going back on my decision." He was taken aback a bit before accepting my decision.

"Do you want me to tell the men, sir?" he said.

"No, I will the next time there's a debrief."

The men took it well and every one of them wished me well in whatever I did in civvy life. My main objective now was to get every one of these men back to the UK without any injuries or deaths but that was going to be too hard as we were under constant attack and there was no way the British Army took a step back; instead, it faced the enemy head on. We did that and up till now on this tour we had had no serious injuries. Head down and get through it, as Billy said many times. Day after day and week after week, I counted down the days till I was back in the UK. Looking at the calendar in the mess one day, I counted ten days to go and as I reached ten a voice interrupted me from behind. "Sergeant Richards, how the fuck are you, cub?"

I know that voice, I said to myself. I turned to see my old mate Andy who I joined up with.

"Fuck me with a big stick; it's Andy. How you doing, my good friend?" He stood tall in front of me looking like a fuckin' hippy. "What the fuck's up with the beard, lad? Did you forget to shave or something?" We hugged like only real men do and then looked embarrassed.

"What's this I hear that you're demobbing in a couple of years?" Bugger, he knows. "I've had enough of it Andy, and the family needs me more than I need this shit. Mary wants to give our marriage another go and well, so do I. Plus, Mummy's not doing well and of course Sammy's death has taken its toll."

He held out his hand to me. "I'm sorry about Sammy; he was a great lad and deserved better in life." Next thing I know he has a flask in his hand.

"Here's to Sammy and all the other lads we lost."

"Cheers Andy!"

Listen Stephen, I need to talk to you about something that just came across my desk and before I say another word to you, I need to know you will not utter another word of this to anyone and I mean anyone 'cause if you do I will rip your fuckin' tongue out. Swear to me you won't, otherwise I'm out the door without another word spoken." This must be bad because Andy would never act towards me like this.

"Fuck me, Andy, you should know me by now, I do and that's why I'm waiting. Okay I promise, lad, and you know I will never let you down." He went quiet and took another gulp from his hip flask.

"One of my units is being ordered back to Hereford tomorrow for a mission in Ulster; now these boys are no ordinary unit. They are only sent in when someone needs to disappear without a trace. They are bad news, and word is they have been sent back to get intel on your brother Billy. Now he must be a major player in something for him to be a person of interest of that level." I was not expecting that and it fuckin' shut me up for a second or two.

"In what way do you mean person of interest, Andy? That could be—" Before I could get 'anything' out of my mouth, he shouted me down like the major would on a bad day. "I don't fucking know and I'm not about to ask fucking questions just to please you. Take my word for it, Stephen, I don't know anymore but if it warranted sending back D squadron it's not good and if I get wind of this coming back to me I will deny everything and throw the blame straight back on you. I will say you asked me for info and I told you to go fuck yourself, it will be that simple." I was dumbstruck. What the hell had Billy gotten himself into?

"Cheers Andy and listen, lad, it's between me and you no matter what." He got up, shook my hand and wished me good luck; that was it. Now my head was spinning. I have ten days left out here and no hope of getting away until then. I needed to make contact and get word to Billy to secretly contact me which was near impossible. I just sat there with my mind going at the rate of a V6. "Fuck, fuck, fuck."

"What's up, sir, you finally losing it." It was Corporal Smithy with his usual banter.

"It's nothing Smithy, I'm just thinking out loud as usual."

"What the fuck with?" he shouted as he left. I was in no mood to answer back even though he was taking the piss. I decided that I had to make contact some way and get Billy to call me from a secure line but who? It hit me, John, speak to John and ask him to tell Billy to call me on this number from a safe line. No one would ever suspect John, he lives miles from home and it worked. Two days later Billy called me from a telephone miles from his home and somewhere they would never expect him to call from. I got my hands on a phone taken from a dead raghead which was never handed in. "Listen, Billy, I'm not staying on this line long so listen carefully. You're being watched, and an SAS squad are on route to gather intel on you. This is deadly serious, boy. You are a 'Person of Interest' to someone. I will be home in two weeks so keep your fuckin' head down and watch your six."

All he said was, "Okay, got it." I rushed back to cover my tracks just in case the call got traced because I could be being watched as well. A week later, the major called me into his office and I thought, *shit I'm done for*, but to my surprise he said the whole squad is being sent back home the next day and our tour was over.

"Job well done, see you on the plane tomorrow." When I told Smithy and the lads, they were elated and every one of us were packed within the hour and got full fuckin' drunk. That plane was not a nice place when we got off it at the other end. Even the major was still drunk. I spoke to the men and told them I would see them in twelve days at base. I headed straight to Mary's and spent the night before traveling onto Belfast. I got a lift with a lorry driver on his way to Londonderry so I wouldn't have Brass pull me in for no reason. He dropped me off in walking distance of the house. I had to make it to the house without anyone knowing so that I could speak to Billy freely 'cause when they knew I was home, things would change quickly. It was 10 p.m. and quiet. I waited in the tractor barn until the next morning, which was a Saturday, hoping Billy would be the first to get to the house to see Mummy. He was. I clicked my cheeks as if to call a dog and he looked round. Luckily, he knew not to raise awareness that I was there because as far as the army was concerned I was still at Mary's. "What the fuck are you involved in, Billy? This is deadly serious."

He looked stunned. "First off, how do you know this?"

No way, I'm not telling him anything. "It came my way, I don't know from who or where but it's fuckin' real and that's all I know. At this moment, there are undercover soldiers watching your every move and when they know I'm home, mine too." He just stood there looking as dumb as fuck at me. "It's not a fucking joke, Billy; what the hell are you involved in?"

He shook his head as if to say, what the fuck are you on about. "Nothing Stephen, absolutely nothing and that's the truth and if I was I would tell you even if you're in the fucking British Army. Seriously look at me, nothing." I didn't know what to think now. "Come on, put your hood up just in case and let's get inside. Mummy will be over the moon to see you, but listen Stephen, she's not good. The treatment has taken its toll on her and we had to bring in some carers so don't for fuck sake show her you're alarmed when you see her."

As we got to the door I tried to look as if everything was great and I was happy to be home. *Good luck with that*, I thought. I went straight upstairs to see Mummy and I wish I hadn't. She looked so bad and near to death. I kept thinking what the hell went so wrong since I was last home. I did my best to act normal and look happy to see her, but I couldn't hold back the tears. Jane was there with her and the look on her face said it all. I just told her I was so happy to be home with my family again. "You look so good, Stephen. I'm glad you're home for good." I looked round at Billy wondering what she was told because me being back home for good was at least two years away.

"Come on, Stephen, your Mummy needs to get dressed and get her treatment. You can catch up a little later," said Jane. I don't think she noticed me leaving; she was that poor.

"Billy, let's go somewhere to have a chat, we need to get a grip on this." Thinking the house could be bugged we made our way up to the attic room where nobody goes. "Right, lad, what I told you is real and immediate, you are being watched and you are a Person of Interest to the security forces which means something is going on. Tell me straight and I promise you it stays up here." He started to show some concern. "Listen lad. I am not involved in anything. I'm a member of the UVF but we have not been active since August last year. I'm not watching anyone or targeting anyone and if in the future I have to, I fuckin' will no matter who's watching me. I'm still fighting a battle too, you know, just like you." I believed him because he was not the sort of man to lie to someone he could trust. What to do now was the problem. "Leave it with me, Stephen. I have a few friends in the PSNI (Police Service of Northern Ireland) that will get me some answers. Give me a day or so to contact them."

Did I just hear right? "You, a UVF man, has a contact in the PSNI? Are you kidding me? Holy fuck, I thought that all ended when the RUC were replaced in 2001. It's like a Hollywood movie for fuck's sake." Well, that made him laugh at least.

"So, what would you call your contact that give you this info about me? The fuckin' postman. You have your sources and I have mine so don't get cocky with me, soldier boy." Shit, he was right.

"Fair dues lad. You're right as usual but it still smells." I left it for now hoping that he get the answers we needed. I spent the next few days with Mummy giving her all the help I could, but I could see that she was going downhill. The strange thing was it seemed she was content with the journey she was taking and did not want or have the will to fight back. It was good to be home and I could show my face now. Every time I left the house, I knew that I was being watched by my brothers in arms and I had to pretend that they were not there. As good as his word, Billy got the info he needed. We again went into the attic to talk about it.

"Well, what did you hear back from your postman"? That lightened the mood a bit. "It turns out I'm the target of the local IRA. Permission was asked of the Belfast command by the Tyrone brigade to take me out. Apparently, I'm a threat to them in this area. Word is if they watch me they might catch them in the act." That changed everything.

"We need to beef up your security then." Just as I said that, Jane shouted up the stairs that there was somebody at the door for me. "We'll talk later; I'd better see who this is." When I reached the door, I nearly choked. Two PSNI police.

"Stephen, we need to have a chat with you if it's possible?" We went into the front room and closed the door. "What's up officer? Have I been called back?" He leaned forward. "Your brother Billy has a marker on him. The local IRA boys want him dead and they got permission from Belfast command. Because you're army, they would love to get you as well and they know you're home. We need to get you both out of here now." Right, that's going to happen.

"Sorry no way. We are not leaving our mum, end of discussion, so you can take your idea and fuck off out the door." That didn't go down well.

"I can have you RTU within the day if I wanted, Sergeant, so don't start to mouth off at me when I'm only trying to help you both." I understood what he was doing but there was no way in hell we were leaving Mummy now.

"Sorry, Officer but no, we are staying. We will work with you, but we are staying put." He sat back in the chair looking despondent and looked at his colleague to see if he could make me see sense. "I don't know if you remember me, Stephen, but I went to school with your brother John so I know the score. How is your mum doing?" I looked at him and tried to work out who he was.

"She's not good, the treatment has not worked, and the cancer is spreading plus Sammy's death last year has not helped matters either. Are you a brother of Davy Jack by any chance?" As soon as I said it, he smiled.

"Yep, you got it, I'm Robert, so now you know me. I'm on your side, but this is serious, these IRA fuckers are animals and will shoot at anything to get to the target. It doesn't help that they are as thick as fuck and I mean stupid cunts as well."

"I understand, Robert, but we were still not moving. Tell you what, we will make it easy for them, draw them out and you guys do the rest. Now I have a funny suspicion you have some boys watching us as we speak so set up a meet with them and we can work together. That's my only offer and yes you can have me sent back, Officer, but Billy is going nowhere, and I would love to see you try." I think Robert understood me. He knew what Billy was capable of.

"Fuck's sake," said the first officer.

"I was told I was wasting my time, but I had to try. Leave it with me and I will let you know."

That night I was in the tractor barn hoping I would have a visitor and sure enough sitting there on the bales of hay was four lads from D squadron SAS. "Sergeant Richards. How are you doing, buddy? Let me introduce the lads, this is one, he's two, that's three and I'm four. We heard a lot about you from a friend. It's nice to finally meet you." I knew right away Andy put them right about me.

"Cold out there, lads, tell you what, make yourself at home and I will get some warm grub for you all." They were nice fellas and knew exactly what the plan would be. According to intel, word was that Billy would be hit on his way to work, most likely Saturday morning when the roads would be clear. "We have to take them alive, if possible, Sergeant. The Shiners (Sinn Fein) would use it to their advantage in the negotiations. It would be Christmas all over again in March for them cunts." The DUP, of course, would use it for their advantage if they were taken out. We didn't have to wait long. The PSNI got word that they planned to hit Billy on Saturday morning. One of the boys from D squadron would take Billy's place driving his van with another one in the back. They even knew where they would attack the van, so the rest of D squad would sneak to that point during the night. Sure enough, at that exact moment three gunmen from the IRA arrived at the spot and got ready to ambush Billy's van. The word was given for the van to leave the house and they had to assume that they were watching the house as well, so they stuck to Billy's routine. As the van approached the ambush spot, the three amigos leapt from the hedge, only to be completely surprised, then taken down with warning shots and commands. They hadn't a hope. One of the terrorists took two rounds to the legs because he swung his weapon around. The other two shit themselves on the spot. The only resemblance these fuckers had to animals was that they shit themselves in a field. It was a job well done, as we say in the battlefield. There was a watcher on the house that the PSNI had tabs on and he was arrested moments later, so four cowardly scumbags arrested and only one casualty that would never walk again. That night, the two PSNI men called at the house to update us and warned Billy that they knew what he was involved in and if they got evidence of any description linking him to any sort of criminality they would not hesitate in arresting him. They got a sharp swift answer. "Good luck with that, sir." I was hoping that we could all now concentrate on Mummy and give her the support she needed to get her well again, but I was so bloody wrong.

Chapter 12
Truth That Leads to Revenge

"So, do you think you will ever come back home again and settle down, Stephen?" That's a question I got all the time when I was home but this time the answer was different.

"Up to now, James, I would always say nope, not a hope in hell but that's now changed with everything going on. I think Sammy's death was the final piece in the jigsaw that changed my mind, but saying that, I think Mummy's sickness had a big say in it as well." That was the first time I voiced my thoughts out loud and it seemed to be welcomed warmly. I've been home now nearly a week and Mummy seems to be getting worse so the fact that I was now going to be based in the UK would help out immensely. I could get home within two hours if need be and the army would go out of their way to help me. It was a Friday morning and James needed to get to the shop and he only called in to see how Mummy was doing. I was up and having breakfast. Of course, he helped himself to some bacon from my plate when he sat down and then helped himself to the tea in the pot. "Help yourself there, cub, here's one I made earlier." We both laughed and he nearly choked on the bacon. "Ha-ha that will teach you." Just as I said that, the back door burst open and scared the shit out of us. It was my turn to choke on the bacon. It was Boyd with a big box. "What the fuck are you doing, boy, I just shit my knickers, you prick." He shoved this large box onto the worktop panting like a mad man who just run a marathon.

"You need to see this. Living room now." We followed him in, wondering what the hell he was smoking. "I was up late last night looking through some of Sammy's stuff trying to sort it out and I came across his video camera. I decided to plug it in and see what he had recorded. You just won't fuckin' believe what he's been up to all these years." That got our attention right away knowing that Sammy spent so much of his time recording things on his cameras. "Billy's on his way." We looked at him waiting for some idea of what the hell he was on about.

"For fuck's sake, Boyd, what?" He took a deep breath and the next thing he said shook us to the core. "All this time we thought Sammy was a fucking alcoholic and just couldn't handle life. Well, fuck me, we were so wrong lads. The whole time he's been trying to find out who killed Daddy. That's what he's been doing all along. He's been pretending to be a wino, a down and out drunk to get information on these fuckers all along." Silence. For a moment we had no words to say.

I eventually swallowed the large lump in my throat, "How do you know that?" I said.

"Watch this." Boyd set up Sammy's video camera and connected it up to the large TV in the living room. It was Sammy sitting in front of the camera doing a video diary and he seemed to be very drunk and over the moon. "I was right, it was them, and I got the fuckers hook, line and sinker. Tonight, in O'Rileys, I heard him admit it. He fuckin said, I killed that gobshit's oul boy and he was laughing like a dirty fucker when he said it but, he fuckin said it." At that point, he stopped and started to get upset and then he started to cry but through the tears he carried on. "After all these years of taking shit from every Fenian cunt around, all the snide remarks and all them fuckers laughing at me, but I have the final laugh and it's all paid off." He took a swig from a bottle of beer. "Right I'm off to tell Daddy the news. Tomorrow, it's taking a long bastard time but we're getting the revenge we swore to on Daddy's coffin." He started to cry so hard we could feel his pain just watching it. After about a minute, he wiped his tears and looked into the camera as if he knew it would be his last entry." That's when he switched of the camera and it dawned on us that he recorded that last clip the night he died. He went up to the graveyard and told Daddy the news just before he fell into that bloody ditch and died on his way home from the graveyard. We were in shock and couldn't believe what we had just seen. As I got up, I said we need to get Billy.

"I'm here, lad." He was standing at the door watching it all. "Are there any more recordings?" Boyd opened the box and showed us dozens of VHS tapes and the same amount of dairies. Luckily, Sammy dated every tape, so we knew what to look at.

"Here, Boyd, try this one. It's the next date going back." Boyd stuck it on and pressed play. Sure enough there was Sammy, drunk as usual in front of the camera.

"I think I know who it was now. I was in O'Rileys last night and the same group of gobshites were mouthing off at me. Sean Murray, Eamon Kelly and Joe and Kevin Burns. They were the same fuckers that gave me a kicking the other month in Omagh but last night they started taking the mickey out of me, thinking I was full drunk. Fuck, I'm a great actor. Joe Burns knocked me down with a punch, then stood over me before kicking me in the chest and putting a make-believe gun with his fingers to my head. Bang bang, just like your Daddy, he said. He was definitely the shooter. Next time I will have proof, don't you worry." You could drive a truck through the house and we wouldn't have noticed.

"Jesus Christ, Jesus fuckin' Christ. All this time we thought that Sammy was a waste of space, but the poor fucker was trying to find out who killed Daddy. Jesus Christ!" James said what we all were thinking and fuck me, we felt sick to the bone, thinking of what he went through and what we said to him and all alone he was killing himself trying to get to the truth. I felt so sick. Next thing, Billy rushed out of the house and got into his car. I ran out and stopped at the front of the car hoping he would stop, well he didn't. I jumped out of the way as he took off, but he stopped almost right away. Mummy was standing at the front door with her hand out, telling him to stop which he did. I knew why Billy was so angry and wanted to go get them. Billy hammered Sammy that day in the barn when he also punched me. He did it because he

164

thought Sammy was hurting Mummy with his drinking. Now he knew different and that upset him.

"Billy, come back in the house please, everyone, back inside now." She didn't know what was going on but just happened to be at the front and heard a commotion.

"Don't say anything to her Billy, she doesn't know." We walked into the kitchen where Mummy was sitting and sat around the table. "I don't know what's wrong, Billy, but please don't fight boys. I don't think I can cope with it." Billy got up and gave Mummy a kiss.

"Sorry, Mummy, I just got a bit annoyed and took it out on the lads. Sorry lads, I'm a bit of a dick sometimes." We all smiled and agreed with him.

"Good boys. Now, I'm a bit tired so I'm off to my room for a rest." We agreed to meet up later to work out where we go from here. At 5 p.m., we all met up in the tractor shed. We all looked stunned and no doubt looking to finish off Sammy's work. "As far as I'm concerned, I intend to get these fuckers and kill them all and if you're not with me you'd better stay the fuck out of my way." One by one, we all answered Billy. I'm with you, lad, was the answer. He left the shed and came back with a green holdall. "I called Jimmy Wright after I left here this morning and got a few bits to do the job. They are clean and untraceable." He pulled out three hand guns and a sawn-off shotgun. "Now I know some of you won't like the idea of this so just say so and I won't mind but I intend to kill them." I walked forward and picked up a hand gun.

"Just the job. This is mine." Boyd picked up the shotgun and James the last hand gun. We were all intent on killing them.

"So it looks like they always meet up in O'Rileys on Wednesday night to play darts and Sean Murray, who's a taxi driver, always waits for them outside to taxi them home."

John came forward. "And how the hell did you find out all that since this morning?" *He's right*, I thought. "Jimmy Wright knew all along what Sammy was doing. He has been watching them for some time for Sammy, he knew all along what he was up to and never said a thing to me, the cunt. But there's more. That's a promise they both made to Mummy, believe it or not."

"Fuck off, Billy, are you telling us Mummy was in on it as well?" He nodded his head yes. "How fucking stupid are we, why the hell did one of us not notice anything?"

Billy got a bit irate and stopped the conversation dead. "So fucking what? What's done is done and now we have a job to do. We have to finish off what poor Sammy started." There was no doubt Billy was taking this hard after what had happened between them in the barn when he went for Sammy not long before his death. I could also see that John was in shock and had his doubts because he kept pacing up and down looking at the floor.

"John, John, look at me, lad. We will understand if you aren't up for this and don't want anything to do with it." That's when the other lads caught on. John was a civil man with strong Cristian beliefs and it wouldn't be right to force him into this. Billy walked over to him putting his hand on his shoulder.

"John, one of us needs to stay here and look after Mummy. She needs one of us around all the time; that's more important than anything else." He shook his head in agreement. "Good man."

We all went over to John and reassured him. "What vehicle are we using?" I asked.

"Don't worry; that's covered. Jimmy Wright got me a transit to use so everything is set. We go for them Wednesday night. Plan is we follow them when they leave the pub which is usually around 11.30 p.m. As we get to the tee junction, this side of the bridge we run them off the road. I will deal with the driver Murray. Boyd, you're the best driver so you're driving, Stephen and James, you're in the back so when I shout, get out the side door and get the two in the back. I will go around the front and get whoever's in the front seat. Remember, I want Joe Burns alive; there are some questions I need answers to, fuck the rest of them. If all goes to plan we get them into the back of the transit and take them to the unused barn out by Grandad's farm. I will check it all out tomorrow to make sure there's nothing to worry about." On Sunday, we went to church but without Mummy for the first time as she was getting so weak and terribly ill. We had prayers said for her during the service but we all knew that it was not good. John and his family came down for the day and we decided not to talk about what had happened in the last few days so to give Mummy all the support she needed. Mary and Rosie flew in from the UK to spend some time with me because she knew there was no way I would be spending my leave away from home. It got to the point where Mummy stayed in her bedroom most of the day because it was more comfortable for her and we made sure she had company when she was awake. That's where the girls took over and made sure everything was in order. When the doctor called in on Monday, he suggested that maybe it was time that we put Mummy in a palliative care home so she would get all the care she needed and that hopefully she would pick up enough to carry on her chemo treatment. Of course, the moment you hear the doctor say that, you straight away think it's to give her the best care until her time has come. "Are you saying there's no hope, Doctor, because if you are she might as well spend her last days at home with us."

He straight away butted in on me. "No, Stephen, I'm not. Your mum has a 50/50 chance of pulling through this but I'm sure you have all noticed she has all but given up. We need to make sure she gets the care and needs to build her strength up because she still has a battle to fight with the cancer." I knew we had to listen to him.

"Stephen, he's right," said Jane. "She gets all the love in the world here but the specialist care she needs, we can't give it to her at home." We all then agreed and Mummy was taken into a care home the next day. All the girls Jane, Grace, Mary and Georgina said that they would be with her around the clock to make sure she had a friendly face when she opened her eyes. Aunty Mary and Aunty Joyce were so good as well. They were never off the phone or calling in with Mummy. It was just a matter of time to see what way it went and we all hoped it was the way back to us. It was Wednesday, and the time had come to end the twenty-five years of hurt. We met up at Grandad D's barn where Billy had stored the transit late evening waiting for confirmation that the fuckers were in O'Rileys. At 8 p.m., a car turned up the lane to the barn. "Shit boys there's a car coming up the lane and they just turned their lights off." Billy looked out the window. "Don't worry, it's Jimmy. He's coming to give the go ahead." Sure enough, Jimmy walked in the door with a grin on his face. "We're on, lads, the three of them are playing darts as usual. If they stick to what they always do, Murray will pick them up just after 11.30 p.m."

"No going back now," I said.

"Good man Jimmy, Listen, when we get the fuckers in the back of the van, we high tail it out of there right away. Jimmy is going to clear up whatever we leave behind so the alarm is not raised by some fucker coming across a bullet-ridden taxi. You all sorted Jimmy?" Jimmy looked at Billy with a fuck yes grin.

"I told you boys at your daddy's funeral that I would help out in anyway and I mean to stick to my word. William looked out for me when I was a young cub so when Sammy told me his plans fifteen years ago I was in all the way. It's just a pity the poor cub is not here to get his revenge. I intend to help you get it for him." Boyd walked forward and looked at us all.

"It's time Daddy and Sammy got their revenge. It's time we ended this." No more words were said. We got into the van and headed off to O'Rileys bar. It was 11.15 p.m. The street was quiet. We all sat in the van without speaking to make sure we didn't raise suspicion. In the dead of night, we would be heard whispering let alone talking. 11.20 p.m.

Billy spoke. We were in the back without a view. "Taxi's just pulled up, it's Murray."

"Shit, shit, shit," James mumbled.

"Listen, James. I've done this many times, so leave the shooting to me. You just have my back and get them in the van when I say. If you think you have to shoot, don't hesitate, double tap to the head. That means two quick shots to the head. Do not shoot to wound, because the fuckers could be armed." He nodded.

"Thanks, Stephen." I could hear a car engine rev up on my left.

"Here we go lads, masks on and hold on." Boyd started up the van and headed off after them. The bridge was about two miles out the road, so I had a good idea of how long it would take us to get there. The adrenalin was high and just like the battles in Iraq. I looked at James and I could tell he was shitting bricks.

"James, James, look at me. When that door opens, make as much noise as you can. Scare the fuck out of them and don't let them think. Got it? Come on, James this is for Daddy and Sammy." That changed his look. I could hear Billy and Boyd in the front getting ready to take them out.

"Here we go, Boyd, make sure I'm in line with the driver's door but give me enough room to get out."

"Right," Boyd shouted. 'Bang Bang'. *Fuck, did we shit ourselves*. It was Billy banging the partition on the inside of the van.

"Hold on, lads," the van swung out to the right before viciously swinging to the left and coming to a halt. The shooting started right away. Billy leaned out the window and fired into the driver's side. I swung the side door open and jumped out with James on my tail. Billy had already taken out Murray in the driver's seat and was making his way around to the passenger's side. I reached for the rear door and screamed, "Out, out, get the fuck out now, move." I grabbed him by the hair and delivered a blow to the back of his head with the butt of the gun. He went down hard, and James followed with a kick to the head. "Get him in the van now. You in the back, out now or I'll blow your fuckin' head off. Move, I said fuckin' move, you fucking piece of shit. Out you cunt." As I dragged him across the back seat, I was still screaming like a mad man at him. I dragged him onto the ground. "James, take him out." Again, James laid him out cold with heavy kicks to his head. We got him in the back with the other fucker. "Tie them up, James." I went around to the front of the taxi and

Billy was beating the face of Joe Burns. It was fucking horrific to see. He was driving punch after punch straight down onto Joe's face screaming at the same time. "Billy, come on we need to go." There was no getting through to him. I pushed Billy off Burns and tried to lift his lifeless body into the back of the transit. "Give me a hand with this fat fucker someone." Billy got his wits about him again and lifted Joe's legs into the van. Boyd and James had secured the other two and did the same to Burns.

"Fuck me, is he even alive, Stephen?" Don't know was my reply, because he was hammered to fuck.

"Right, come on, time to go."

"What about Murray?" Boyd shouted.

"Fuck him. He's dead. Jimmy will sort him out," shouted Billy. We all got into the van and raced off back to the barn. The last thing we needed was a local to come upon us.

Chapter 13
Revenge That Leads to Truth

Nearly twenty-five years after Daddy was shot dead by the IRA, we finally had the chance to have our revenge on the men who took his life and destroyed ours in the process. I was sitting in the back of the van with James, wet, cold and not believing what we just did. I had three IRA men out cold at my feet. Three men that were about to pay for all the pain they inflicted on us. The fourth was back in the taxi dead as a dodo. The van slowed down to a stop before I heard Billy get out and a gate open. Boyd pulled in and stopped to let Billy close the gate and get on board again. "Lights off, Boyd, and don't use your brakes. Use the hand brake if you have to. Those brake lights can be seen for miles out here." We came to a stop and the side door opened right away. "Right, let's get them out." I could tell that Billy was eager to get this done and done quick. We got the three of them inside and tied them all upright to cow rails. We all stood back and made sure we were all okay and not hurt. It had just gone midnight. The whole thing took less than an hour. One hour to capture the fuckers but it took twenty-five years to catch them.

"Jesus Christ, what have we just done?"

"Don't worry, James," said Billy. "This won't take long." We got the three of them conscious and waited until they knew what was going on. Joe Burns was beat to fuck and took longer to come around. "Wake up, you fuckers, time to meet your maker and I'm happy to say he's not fuckin' wearing white. Joe, Joe, wake up, Joe." They all realised that they were about to die and started to beg for their lives. Billy walked up to Joe Burns taking his mask off, "Do you know me Joey boy?

171

Look into my eyes, Joe; it's not the first time you have looked into my eyes, is it, Joe? The last time you looked into my eyes you winked at me and then put two bullets in my daddy's head. Do you know my face now, Joe? I want to be the last thing you see before I put two bullets in your head." He raised his head and looked at Billy's face. The blood was blinding him and most of his teeth were in the back of the van. "I should have killed you as well, you orange b—" Before he said the word 'bastard', Billy drove his knee into his chest.

"Sorry, I never got that, Joe. What did you say?"

"Leave him alone, you orange bastard," shouted Joe's brother, Kevin. I walked towards him and aimed two solid punches to his jaw.

"I think it's better if you keep your mouth shut, fuck-face. Your time will come soon enough."

"Fuck you," he said to me with blood dripping out of his mouth.

"O look Joe, your wee brother is worried about you." At this point, Billy was standing by the side door and picked up a pick-axe. As he walked back to them he turned the pick-axe upside down and removed the shaft. "So, you want us to leave poor Joe alone, do you, Kevin? After all, you, Sean, Joe and wee Eamon here took my daddy's life and you want me to just leave you alone, do yea? Right, that's going to bloody happen." Before I could blink, Billy took a swing at Kevin Burns's legs and smashed his knee cap to shit. The sound of his bones smashing was unreal. Then, another to the other knee cap. The screams of him would wake the dead and look on his face was enough to make you puke. His screams faded away, but he was still screaming. All the air in his lungs was gone. The blood started to trickle out his nose and the snots and slabbers covered his face. It looked like his eyes were about to pop out. Billy just kept swinging at his feet, legs and torso with every bone he made contact with being smashed to pieces.

"Stop it, you fucking bastards. Enough, leave him alone, you orange pricks."

"Shut your mouth, Kelly."

"Fuck you," he shouted back at Boyd. Eamon shouldn't have opened his mouth because Boyd stepped forward and without hesitation put a bullet right between his eyes. He then screamed at him in a rage, "I said, shut your fuckin' mouth, Kelly." We stood there looking at Boyd wondering where the hell that all came from. "What? Do you think because I have no memories of Daddy I don't feel the pain this bunch of murdering bastards put on us? Just because I was only three when it happened doesn't mean I didn't take the same vow as you did at Daddy's grave. I made that vow at Daddy's grave on my tenth birthday." There was no need for us to wonder anymore.

Billy turned to Joe and got his attention again. "This is what it feels like to watch one of your own die in front of your eyes." He turned to his brother Kevin and raised the pick-axe handle. "Your time has come, Kevin; Eamon's pining for company in hell." As he took the first swing, Joe shouted stop. It was a bit late. His forearm smashed in two, sending bone fragments through his skin. "Stop, stop it, leave him alone, please, no more, let him die, please. If you leave him be, I will tell you something you don't know. Just let him be." That got our attention. At first, I thought he was only playing for time hoping that Kevin would bleed to death before Billy could inflict any more pain.

"Sorry Joe, there's nothing I need from you now. I don't want you to say sorry or fucking beg for forgiveness or any other crap. You're about to meet your maker and have a reunion with your brothers in arms, or should I say arm 'cause Kevin just lost one of his."

James stepped forward. "Hold on, Billy; I want to hear what he's got to say. Kill the fucker when he tells us." I agreed with James and so did Boyd. "Okay lads. It's not as if what he has to say will save him. He's brown bread no matter what he comes out with. Come on Joe, out with it. What have you got to say that would make me stop taking your brother to fucking pieces?"

He tried to look up but the beating he had taken was so brutal, he couldn't. Boyd grabbed him by the hair and lifted his face up. "This better be good, because if it's a pile of shit just to stop Billy beating him, it's going to be ten times worse. There's a new chainsaw sitting over there with Kevin's name on it." I looked over and could see nothing that looked like a bow saw let alone a fuckin' chainsaw. *Mind games*, I said to myself.

"You have thirty seconds to impress me, Joe," said Boyd.

"Okay, promise me you'll stop first?" Yea yea right.

"Okay. Promise, Joe. You now have twenty seconds." Billy pulled a bale of hay up to sit on. "We didn't do it alone. We were ordered to kill your Da; we were just carrying out orders."

Both Billy and Boyd stood up and went over to him. "What do you mean, Joe? Answer me, what the fuck do you mean?"

This changes everything, I thought.

"I got an order from the IRA commander in Tyrone to take out everyone in the car no matter who it is." Billy got up in anger and grabbed the pick handle as if to go at Kevin again. "No don't, stop, stop. Fuck. The man who give me the order to take you out is known to you all. You fuckin' know him so you do. He's the one you should be talking to."

"What do you mean? Tell me you cunt, tell me or god so help me I'll swing on him till he sings the sash." said Billy.

"Paddy Connell. Paddy Connell, you're uncle. He's the man who gave the order to take you out"."

We all stopped dead in our tracks. *That can't be right. He must be bullshitting us. We just couldn't take it in. He always helped us out and was there for us*, I kept saying to myself. Billy dropped the pick handle in shock and just kept staring at the ground. Boyd and James walked away trying to take it in. Me? My shock quickly turned to anger. I picked up the pick handle and set about Joe as hard and as brutal as I physically could. His screams filled the barn and I didn't give a shit. I just kept shouting 'fuck you' over and over again as I tore his body apart. Billy then stepped in and stopped me. "Enough, Stephen, enough, it's done." As I stood there out of breath, covered in blood and hardly able to move Billy walked up to him, and just as Joe did to Daddy, put a bullet in his lifeless body. As I sat down, Boyd reached over and took a knife I had in my belt and cut Kevin's throat from ear to ear before James finished him off. He emptied the rest of his mag into Kevin's shaking body. We all did not know what to say or do after that. Even though we just got the revenge we craved for twenty-five years, it felt like nothing had changed.

Just then, Jimmy Wright walked into the barn and we didn't even notice. We were still trying to take in what Joe Burns had just said. "Everybody okay, lads? How did you, holy fuck? What the fuck happened to whoever the fuck that is hanging over there?" He just spotted what was Kevin Burns. No one answered him. "What's wrong, lads? What's happened? James, what's up?" James looked at him with an empty stare. Pointing at Joe Burns, Billy answered him. "He just told us who gave the order to kill Daddy."

Jimmy looked bemused. "Who? Who is it?"

"Paddy Connell," said James.

"Paddy fucking Connell? Your uncle Paddy Connell? Sweet Jesus. Your dad told me never to trust that man. He always said he was a dangerous sneaky fucker. Now we know he was right." The fact that we were standing in a barn with three dead men, covered in blood and all armed never crossed our minds. That's how much of a stupor we were in. "Come on, we need to get this place cleared out before its daylight. Get these fuckers in the van so I can get rid of them. We can talk about that sneaky cunt later." We put what was left of them in the transit, so Jimmy could get rid of them. "Is that everything, weapons and all?"

"Yes, that's it all," Boyd shouted.

"Hey Jimmy, what happened to Murray and his taxi?" He stopped and looked around at me.

"Taxi will be in bits by tomorrow and Murray's in the bog with some of his long-lost mates. That's where I'm taking these piles of shit now and I haven't much time, so I will see you later on at the house." He drove off leaving us to clear any evidence he left behind. It was dawn before we finished and got home. As we all sat around the kitchen table drinking something a bit stronger than tea, we were not able to speak of what just happened.

"Make sure you all destroy your clothes and wash yourselves down well, lads. If they find the bodies they will most likely come here first, so get it done before you leave."

"Okay, Billy."

Before we got up to leave, Mary appeared in the doorway. "Can you lot not keep it down in here? I can hear you all the way upstairs. Well, at least it looks like you lot had a good night?"

That was an understatement.

Chapter 14
Revenge at a Cost

How the fuck do we deal with this? I was standing in the shower at 6 a.m. washing the blood and body parts off me that belonged to the men who killed Daddy in 1979. The shower tray was full of red water and bits of bone fragments. My hands were shaking, and my legs were like jelly as I tried to come to terms with what had just happened and even more so, what was about to happen. Earlier on in the day, I was hoping that today was the day it was all going to end, and we could get on with our lives. That was not going to be, and my hopes just disappeared. The one thing that entered my mind, however, brought me out of the trance I was in. One more to go, just one more and it's over. When I finished up in the shower, I lifted a bottle of bleach and made sure I cleaned every single bit of it just in case the police found out what we did. I took all my clothes out to the barn and burnt the lot. As I walked outside, I looked over at James' house and there was a trail of smoke coming from his garden. *Wonder what he's up to*, I thought. We agreed to meet up later on in The Cross Inn to see where we go from last night's revelations but for now it was time to catch up with Mary and spend some time with my daughter Rosie. There was no way I was going to tell Mary what had happened because she would not take kindly to me bringing trouble to our door with little Rosie here. We just talked about Mummy and how she was doing. It was plain to see that she was losing the battle and just did not have the will to fight on.

"I spent a few hours with your mum yesterday, Stephen, and I think you should be prepared for the worst. She's going downhill very fast and nothing the doctors are doing seems to work with her. They have her on morphine now just to make her comfortable." That was something I didn't need to hear now. "This has all happened since poor Sammy died and it has been in free fall ever since. It's sucked the life and the will to live out of her, so it is."

John and James joined us at the table and we decided to spend the rest of the day with Mummy. When we got to the home to see Mummy, Billy and Boyd were already there. The look on their faces said it all and we just knew that maybe Mummy's time had come. Billy got us some free time together in one of the quiet rooms, so he could update us on how she was doing. "Listen lads, Mummy has given up and there's no fight left in her. I had a good talk with her this morning and she told me Sammy's death was just too much to take. She also told me that she knew what he was up to trying to find Daddy's killers and felt like she was partly responsible for his death." I did think that Sammy's death got to her but taking the blame, shit.

"You haven't told her about the other night, have you?" Billy gave Boyd a bit of a look as if to say, I'm not that fuckin' stupid. "She knows nothing, and it will stay that way for now, right?" We all agreed. "Let's all focus on Mummy for now and we can talk about the other later." We spent the day in with Mummy and she seemed to be in good form, but the morphine was the only thing helping her through. In the evenings, the girls would be with her and made sure she had everything. She had so many visitors and at one point, Jane and Mary said no more. It was getting to the point that she would fall asleep just after saying hello to someone and we would find people just sitting there waiting for her to wake up, not wanting to cause a fuss.

It was now Saturday, three days after we got the fuckers who killed Daddy and people were beginning to talk about the disappearance of four well-known men in the area. Luckily, we had not heard from the PSNI and why should we because as far as we were concerned we didn't know them. That Saturday evening, we got word from Jimmy that the car was gone and would never be found and that the four IRA men were now worm food, but he did have some news that made us change our plans. He also found out that Uncle Paddy would be using a private room for a meeting at his local bar and that it was the perfect chance to confront him. We had two hours to talk it over and if we did go, how we would do it. We sat at the kitchen table as we had done many times before and tried to agree on what to do. Every one of us agreed that we had to do something and sitting on our asses doing nothing was not an option. Do we just burst in and kill the bastards, or do we find Paddy and have it out with him? My point was that if he's been lying to us for twenty-five years about it he would have no problem in lying to us if we asked him the question to his face. We decided that we would have to speak to him and, if need be, beat the shit out of him to get the truth. Billy was up for that as he never liked him and knew through his contacts that he was indeed an IRA man. That was it, we go for him tonight. Kidnap him and interrogate him to find out the truth. It all sounded so easy, but in reality, we all knew it could go very wrong. Word from Jimmy was that they would be meeting around 9 p.m. and there could be up to six people there. Boyd knew the place and informed us that there was a back door leading to a hallway where the room was. It meant that we didn't have to go through the bar which would be full of potential witnesses and also IRA men. We go in and ask Paddy to follow us outside for a chat. If he was innocent, he would agree, and if he wasn't, he would most likely get aggressive. Sitting around the table waiting and watching the clock was unbearable. It felt like it was going backwards and just dragged and bloody dragged. "Right, let's go," said Billy. "John, we need you to drive and we can take my car. It's bigger and got somewhere to throw him in case it goes tit's up. You stay in the car with the engine running, we'll go in and get him and if anyone has a go, take no prisoners lads. Jimmy, you go in first because he will most likely be happy to see you and offer you a drink. Boyd, you're next in the door, then Stephen I will be the last in. If it kicks off, go in hard, fast and don't stop until it's done. I intend to go straight at him so don't get in my way. Right, all set lads?"? We all said yes. "Time to end this, boys. For Daddy, Sammy, Mummy and us, it ends tonight no matter what." The car was very quiet but only because we knew what we had to do. As we got to the bar we could see that there weren't many cars in the carpark so hopefully that meant that there weren't many punters in the bar. "Pull up here, John, facing the exit and keep the engine running. Ready, boys?" Billy shouted; we were more than ready. The back door was open and nobody around, so far so good. We could hear voices inside the room and it sounded like five of six voices.

"Ready?" I asked. "Let's go." James opened the door and entered nice and calm as if he was joining the meeting, with Boyd behind him, then me. As I walked in, I could see Paddy at the end of the small bar with his beer raised as if to say come on lads and have a drink. That look soon changed when Billy followed me in. Billy would never in a million years be seen in this sort of bar. A Republican bar. There would only be one reason for Billy to go into such a bar and Paddy knew it. The look on his face went from hello lads to fuck me. To me, it was the look of guilt and as I thought it, Billy said it. "Get the bastard," Billy shouted. Right away, it went wrong. A bar stool come at us from the corner where Paddy was, we ploughed through whoever was there, hammering the shit out of them. James went left and Boyd to the right. Billy and I went straight up the middle and took out the first man coming our way. James took his man out, no problem, and Boyd, like the whippet he is, made short work of his. I had a bigger fight on my hands with a monster of a man with ginger hair and a beard to match. He just kept swinging at me with haymakers, missing me every time, but I still couldn't stop him. James side-swiped him with a left hook and put him on his ass before I knocked him cold with two boots to the head. He was going nowhere. The barman appeared with a Hurley stick and swung at Billy connecting with his shoulder. I drove at him with a side kick to his head and he went down. I stomped on him until he showed no movement or life. Billy was full on with two men who seemed to be protecting Paddy and knew how to handle themselves, but they were no match for him. He dropped the two of them and then we all piled in to them. The four of us turned on them and left them for dead, then a shot rang out. We looked up and Paddy's son, our cousin Seamus, stood there with the smoking gun in his hands. We all picked up whatever we got our hands on and directed it a Seamus, bottles, stools, and glasses. Anything we could use, it went his way. Paddy, Seamus and the younger brother, Martin, high-tailed it out the door leaving us to finish off whoever was left. It didn't take long. The side door we came through burst open shoving the tables that blocked it out of the way. It was John.

"Come on quick; Paddy and two others are getting away in a car." If they got away, it would be bad. Paddy would have every IRA man after us with orders to kill us all.

"Come on, he's getting away," I shouted. We all took a bit of a beating but were able to get up and out the door pretty sharpish. I looked behind to make sure we had all got out okay when I spotted Billy struggling to keep up. "Dirty rotten bastard. Fuck, fuck, fuck," Billy shouted.

"Come on, Billy, we need to go." Something was not right with him. I helped him to the car and we took off the direction they went. Boyd said he had a good idea what road they took so John put his foot down. "You all right, Billy?" I shouted.

"No, I'm fucking not, some fucker just shot me, bastard, keep going, I'm okay."

"Let me see," I shouted. He had a gunshot wound to the belly. "We need to get Billy to the hospital."

"Just keep going, for fuck's sake," Billy shouted. Boyd was giving directions to John hoping that we were right and then we saw tail lights.

"There they are; they just went round the bend; faster, lad." At this point, Billy was still bleeding and had lost a lot of blood. "Christ sake, keep still, Billy, I think we have it stopped, don't worry, we have this." We got closer and closer until, all of a sudden, the rear lights disappeared. "Shit, where the fuck did they go? Fuck, keep a lookout both ways, they could have turned up a lane."

As we got to the next corner, Boyd spotted a red light in the hedge on the other side of the road. "There, I seen a red light down there, slow down, I think they've crashed." As we stopped, we could see from our headlights a figure crawling out of the hedge.

"There, in the hedge," I shouted. "Stop, John, stop, and keep the lights on them." We all piled out of the car, only to find Paddy on his hands and knees and cut to shit on the road. "Check the car, Boyd," I shouted. "And watch out, they have a gun." I walked over to Paddy who was now sitting on his ass in the middle of the road; he was wet, covered in blood and muck from the field. Before long, James and John stood beside me and Boyd was making his way back from the wrecked car. "They are both still alive but not for long. Keep back 'cause there's a fierce smell of petrol and it could go up anytime. Give me your knife, Stephen," said Boyd.

I looked at the car and said, "No, hold on a minute."

"Fuck it, it's time we finished this off, Stephen." All of a sudden, the shadow of the car lights that were lighting us up broke. We turned around to see Billy trying to stand at the front of the car, but he couldn't. He had lost too much blood and was very weak.

"Stephen, Stephen, bring that cunt over here," Billy shouted. Boyd and John grabbed Paddy and dragged him screaming over to the front of the car. Through the bright lights of the car that were blinding Paddy, he started to beg for his life. We all just stood there listening to him cry like the bitch he was and all he had to say was, "I'm sorry, I'm sorry." Well, we didn't give a fuck if he was sorry or not. Billy started to breathe heavy as he tried to speak. "Because of you, our daddy's dead. It was you all along and you even had the fucking gall to carry his coffin; you carried the coffin of a man you just condemned to death, you sick murdering bastard. Well, I was the last person Daddy saw before he died, you're about to do the same thing, Paddy. Enjoy hell." Without hesitation, Billy lunged forward and grabbed him by the face, ramming both his thumbs into his eye sockets and he squeezed as hard as he could with Paddy screaming like hell. He squeezed until his eyes popped in his skull. Billy would indeed be the last thing Paddy ever saw. He had his revenge at last. Billy looked at me and nodded.

"Pick this piece of shit up," I said. "It's time to meet your maker like the other fuckers, Paddy, and as I said to the bastards that pulled the triggers, he will not be wearing white." Jimmy and Boyd got him on his feet. "You're about to get a taste of hell on earth Paddy and you can have your two sons as company." They dragged him screaming, crying and begging for his life to the wreckage of the car and rammed him in through the broken window at the back.

"Stephen," Billy shouted. I turned around to find him taking a lighter out of his pocket; "Burn the fuckers" I looked him in the eyes, grabbed the lighter; "With pleasure." It was time to end this. I walked up to the car, flicked the lighter and sent them all to hell. We had no time to stand and gloat because Billy was in bad shape. "Get him in the car; we need to get him to hospital." We took off leaving behind the past where it now belonged, in the past.

We knew it was bad, but we also knew that Billy was as tough and hell. "We're nearly there Billy, just a few more miles to go." Boyd was driving like hell and not giving a shit about anyone else on the roads. James and I were in the back with Billy trying to keep him talking but it was no good.

"He's not breathing, Stephen. Come on, Billy, talk to us lad, talk to us." As we got to the edge of the town the bright lights of the roads lit the car up and we could see his face. He was lifeless and hardly fit to breath. His eyes would open up now and then, but close just as quick.

"We're here," Boyd shouted. We stopped outside A&E to get him out of the car, but at that stage, we all knew he had gone too far. He opened his eyes, looked around at us all and smiled.

"We did it lads, we did it."

We all put our hands on his chest, "Yes, we did, Billy." He was gone. Billy died with all his brothers around him. As the staff rushed out they got him on the trolley, but we knew it was too late. They tried their best, but it felt like he wanted to go and take his place beside Daddy, Mummy and Sammy. Billy died on the 4th of April 2004. 8,888 days after Daddy's death. The actions of the IRA that day back in 1979 claimed its last victim.

Chapter 15
Saying Goodbye Again

We spent most of that night and the next morning in police custody explaining what happened. Courtesy of James, we all knew what to say and we all knew if we stuck to his story we would get through this and get back to our families and, more importantly, Mummy. Because of me being in the army, the PSNI officer spoke to me first with a reprehensive of my Unit. "So, Stephen, you know why you're here don't you?" I replied I do. "In your words, I want you to tell me what happened tonight that lead to the fight in the bar and then led to your brother's death by a gunshot"?

I just stuck to the story. "Well, I was due to go back to the base the following day so we all decided to go out for a drink. Just us five lads, none of the wives. We walked into the pub."

"Why that pub, Stephen? Why did you all decide to go in there?" I just kept saying to myself, *stick to the story.*

"Uncle Paddy said to us on many occasions that if we were ever in the area to pop in for a chat and a pint. He would often ask us to call in for a pint. As we walked in, Uncle Paddy was at the end of the bar in the far corner. We didn't know for sure he was going to be there that night, but he was. He lifted his glass to us and called us over, but for some bloody reason, halfway across the pub we were set upon by up to eight men, it could have been more, I don't know. We just fought like fuck to get out of there. We got the best of them and were about to get the hell out of there when someone pulled a gun and shot Billy. I didn't see who it was because I was hammering the face of the bar man who just levelled Billy with a Hurley stick, and I didn't know at the time if or who was shot, I only found out Billy was shot when he couldn't get up. I rushed over and helped him up. We got him out the door as fast as we could and into the car. At that point they were still coming at us with bar stools, glasses and whatever the hell they could lay their hands on. We went straight to A&E to get Billy help, but it was too late. I'm sure you know the rest."

"Did you know that your Uncle Paddy was involved in a car crash just after leaving the bar during the fight?" I shook my head no and tried to look puzzled. "Paddy and two of his sons who were in the car were killed. The three of them burnt to a cinder." Again, I acted shocked and lost for words. "We found a forty-five revolver in the car and it could have been the weapon used to shoot Billy, which means someone in that car could be the person who murdered your brother."

"Jesus Christ," I said. I was still trying to look shocked which didn't take much as I was still trying to come to terms with losing yet another brother. "I don't know what to say, Officer; my brother Billy's murder has not sunk in yet." At that point, the officer stopped the tape, closed his notes and told me he was letting us go, but that until a full investigation was completed, I was being released into the custody of the Army. As we made our way out to the front, I met James, Boyd and John waiting for me. We had all been interviewed at the same time. We were all released at the same time. "Let's go home lads."

Sitting around the kitchen table as we did many times we tried to make sense of the night before. Where there was six, now there was only four. Sammy died trying to find out who killed Daddy and Billy died killing the men who killed Daddy. The two boys whose lives were destroyed that faithful morning back in 1979 finally gave their lives for revenge in 2004. Even though we finished off what Mummy made us swear to on Daddy's coffin, we now had to tell her it was done, but it was our revenge at a cost. How could we tell her just before she died that she had lost another son. We decided to keep it from her. As we made our way into her room where she was being cared for by Mary, Jane and Georgina, we could tell it wasn't going to be long for her. The four of us sat around her bed and let her know we were there. "Hello boys, I knew you'd be here soon."

James lent forward so she could hear every word he said. "Mummy, it's done, you have your revenge."

She turned to him and said, "I know darling, Billy told me." That took us back a bit. She looked around at us all with tears and a strange look of happiness in her eyes, "I am so proud of you all my lovely boys, I will miss you all, but it's time for me to be with William and the boys. I want to go home to be with my darling William." Mummy died on the 5th of April 2004 with her sons around her. We truly believe that when Billy died, he visited Mummy that night in her dreams and told her of her revenge. That's why she died happy knowing she could have the last laugh. She died knowing it was all done for the love of a father.